The Devil Wears Timbs V

A Novel by Tranay Adams

Chapter One

Fear was ripping up the road going eighty-five miles an hour and leaving debris in his wake. His face held a stern expression and he gripped the steering wheel, foot mashing the gas pedal further and further. His mind was consumed with all of the shit that he had gone through with Anton and Eureka. He couldn't help but think how he had deceived them in keeping away from them that he was the one that had murked their father and their mother was the one that had paid him to do it. The more he thought about all that had happened between them, the more his heart ached. In losing them he had lost the family that he'd yearned for since the passing of his own. If he could do something that could change everything that had happened up to the point where he had pulled that trigger and killed their father, then he would do it. No questions asked.

Things were just the way that they were and he was going to have to learn how to cope with them. Otherwise, his demons were going to eat him alive.

Boof!

Fear snapped out of his daydream and looked alive. He looked to the front passenger seat and found a frowning Raymar there. His facial expression was a questioning one.

"What was that?" he inquired.

"I think one of the back tires is blown."

"Fuck," he slammed his fist down on the steering wheel. Next, he pulled over to the side of the street and threw open the door, jumping out. He made his way to the back of the vehicle and saw that the back tire on the passenger side was flat. He changed the tire and when he went to slam the trunk he noticed a flashing red dot just below it. A line creased his forehead and he took it off of the car, looking at it closely trying to figure out what it was. That's when it dawned on him that what he was holding was a tracking device. Soon after, he realized that Anton had put it there. Hearing someone speeding at his rear, he shot to his feet and whipped around. He saw Anton coming straight at him on a motorcycle with the sun rising over the horizon.

"Shit, it's him, we've gotta get outta here!" Raymar hollered out of the window. For a time Fear stood there not saying anything, just watching his enemy speeding in his direction. "Did you hear me, man? We've gotta go!"

"So leave!" he told him without turning around.

"What?" he frowned up.

Fear whipped around and said, "I said, leave, get the fuck from up outta here. The GPS is set for the airport and there's a gun in the glove box. I have faith that you'll get there safely."

Raymar looked away and took a deep breath. He then looked back to the hit-man saying, "Are you sure?"

"Yeah, I'm sure." he gave him a nod.

Raymar threw up a fist and he returned the gesture. With the pleasantries exchanged, the Brazilian native climbed over into the driver's seat and resurrected the Honda. He revved up the vehicle and took off.

Shhhhhhhh!

Anton swung his motorcycle sideways and it skidded to a halt. He kicked up his kickstand and pulled off his helmet, sitting it on the handlebar. He dismounted his bike and stood ten feet away from Fear. He mad dogged him and clenched his fists.

"I've been waiting for this for a looooooong time." he cracked the knuckles on both of his hands.

"You won't be satisfied 'til you kill me, huh?" Fear asked a serious question.

"You mothafucking right," Anton glared at him.

"Well, you'll get no fight from me, lil' brotha," he assured him. "So, you gone have to do what chu gotta do." He removed his jacket and pulled off his shirts, leaving himself bare chest.

"Deep down inside you've been a pussy all of this time? I find that hard to believe, big brotha." he stripped down to his bare chest. Now both men were naked from the neck down. They observed one another's muscular forms and noticed that they resembled each others with all of their old wounds.

"Never a pussy, you know betta than that."

"Indeed I do, but this thing right here isn't going to be one sided," Anton's finger jabbed at the ground. "You're gonna fight me like a mothafucking man, right here and right now!"

"If you think killing me is going to make you feel better, then go ahead!" Fear urged his hot-headed protégé, sticking out his chin and crossing his wrists at his back.

"No! You fight me like a fucking man!" Anton slammed his fist against his chest hard, gritting. "Shoot me the fair one, may the realest killa win!"

"No. I love you too much to kill you, baby boy." His eyes became glassy, but his face was chiseled out of stone. "I regret the day I ever…"

"Shut uuup!"

Bwock!

A spin kick to the jaw sent his mentor's head whipping around, speckles of blood flying every which way.

"Ooof!" he crashed to the ground on his side, mouth bloody, teeth red, eyes blinking as if he was having trouble focusing his vision.

"No. no. no, I don't wanna hear that bullshit! Fuck your love!" he screamed on him, spittle flying from his lips. "Get cho bitch ass up and fight me like a goddamn man, you fucking coward! Show me the killa that the streets feared and my sister loved!"

"No." Fear shook his head and spat blood on the surface, a length of red saliva hanging from his bottom lip. He winced as he got to his booted feet, wrists still crossed at his back. "I love you, and I'm willing to die for you, right here and right now if it means you finding peace."

"Fight meeeee!" Anton shrilled like a madman, red webs in his eyes and veins pulsating on his neck and temples.

"Nooooooo!" The assassin yelled at the top of his lungs, matching his intensity. His eyes stretched wide open, spit clinging to his lips.

"Grrrrr!"

Crack! Crackk! Bwhrack! Thrwack! Shrack! Bwap!

Anton's blows came swift and hard, impacting his old teacher's face and body. Gashes opened on the seasoned killa's cheeks, a knot swelled on his forehead and his nose broke, leaving a sore red line. He dropped to the ground several times but kept getting back up to take the punishment he felt that he deserved. The younger killa drew his fist back and got ready. He watched Fear attentively as he slowly got to his feet, trying to regain his equilibrium. As soon as the executioner had both feet planted firmly on the ground, he did one of those famous Jean Claude Van Damme kicks, whipping his head around in a blur.

Waaap!

The youngster landed back on his feet in a fighting stance just as his opponent hit the surface. His gloved fists were bloody. His face was speckled with blood. His heart was raging inside of his chest. "Haa! Haa! Haa! Haa! Fight…fight me…" he said out of breath, exhausted but determined.

"N…no," Fear breathed with his head angled against the ground. His hard breathing blew debris from under him as he struggled to get to his feet on wobbly legs, holding his wrists in place. His right eye was swollen shut and the size of his nose had doubled, blood dripping from his bottom lip. The League of Executioners lead assassin was hurting more than he'd ever hurt before, but not from his wounds. Nah, he'd caused one of the people he loved most in life a great deal of

4

pain. To him that ranked up there with betrayal, and under L.O.E's law he had to be sentenced to death.

"Come onnnn!" Anton bellowed, with eyes filled with turmoil and pain. He loved the nigga he was putting hands on like a brother, but his deceiving had crippled him emotionally. He'd given him a father figure to love and just like that he snatched it away. This only proved to him that life was a cold-hearted bitch without a conscience. Damn!

Fear spat on the ground and shook his head no, holding his chin up for his successor to take another shot at him.

"I said, no, now finish me!" He closed his eyelids and tears came bursting out of his eyes. His tears weren't ones of physical pain but emotions. He wished that the strapping young hit-man before him could feel all of the love he had in his heart for him. Somehow he thought that by letting him beat him to a bloody pulp would knock some sense into him, but so far the taste of blood had only stir awake the killing machine. With that plan having failed, he could only hope that with him losing his life that his pupil could live the rest of his in peace.

"I love you, lil' homie, and I hope with my death you find some sort of tranquility in life."

"Then you die!" he hissed with a scowling face, baring his teeth.

Bwap! Bwapp! Crack! Bwhrack! Bwop!

Fear fell to the ground with a thud with his good eye nearly closed shut and the side of his face now swelling like he'd been bitten by a poisonous snake. Anton approached him slow and steady, keeping his keen eyes on him. He watched as he wheezed. His face resembled bloody hamburger meat. It was safe to say that he was on his way out.

Anton cracked his knuckles as he advanced in his mentor's direction. He was so focused on him that he was incoherent to the Chevy Impala driving up behind him. It came to a screeching halt at his rear and the driver side door flew open. The vengeful killa grabbed the man that had been as good as family to him by his throat and pulled him forward. Staring into his eyes and studying the pain in his face, he drew his hand back in an Eagle's Claw. With this deadly move that he'd been taught by him, one could tear a man's throat out.

"Antonnn!" Eureka screamed and ran as hard as she could, tears misting in her eyes.

Anton's head snapped over his shoulders and he saw his sister coming up from behind him. "Stay back, Reka!" he shouted her a warning. He then turned his hateful eyes back on the man that he'd been training to kill for years.

"I…I love you, lil' brotha…and I'm sorry for breaking your…your heart." Fear croaked, ready to embrace death like the brave man that he was.

"Don't do it, Ant! You can't!" his sister screamed at his back, still running in his direction.

"Do it, finish me." Fear closed his eyes, tears steadily flowing. He wore a smirk on his lips. It was about to be over and his little brother's soul could finally rest.

Anton's eyes welled up with tears and spilled down his cheeks, running over his lips. His hand slightly shook as he was drawing all of his strength into it for the Kill Move. Truthfully, he didn't want to do it, but this mothafucka had stolen his father from him. In his mind this had to be done. It was the right thing to do. He couldn't turn back now and set him free. Nah, fuck that, how could he live the rest of his life knowing that he'd let the nigga live that had murked out his old man? It would haunt him until the end of his days, so he had to put this issue to bed now.

"Grrrr!"

"Anton, please, you can't kill him!" Eureka slowed to a jog she was so exhausted. She wanted so badly to stop but had to keep going if she was going to save Fear.

The young assassin's head whipped around to his sister, but he still kept his Eagle's Claw above his head. "Why, huh?

Give me one good goddamn reason why I shouldn't rip this cold hearted bastard's throat out!"

"Because…he's Kingston's father."

"King's father? But how is that possible?" Anton asked, forehead deepening with creases. Still holding his Eagle's Claw above his head, he looked back and forth between Eureka and Fear. Tears were sliding down his sibling's cheeks and the man he used to love like a big brother looked pained and defeated.

Flashback

The gravel crunched beneath the tires of Fear's vehicle as he pulled inside of the parking lot of the motel, bright head-lights shining on the nearby units of the establishment. The engine died along with the headlights and the driver side door opened. The killa stepped out toting his briefcase and looking around as he adjusted the collar of his coat. He didn't waste any time procuring a room at the motel from the Indian clerk sitting behind the desk of the place. About five minutes later, Fear came pushing the glass door of the establishment open and heading back to his vehicle. Sitting his briefcase on the roof of the car, he unlocked the backdoor and put both of the dogs on leashes. He slammed the door shut once he'd gotten them out and tied them up to the rear of his ride. This way they could act as guard dogs and protect his domain while he slept. He knew as soon as a mothafucka got too close that they were going to make mincemeat out of his ass.

After playing with the Rottweilers for a time, Fear grabbed his briefcase from off the roof of the car and opened the door of his room. He flicked the light switch on and gave birth to a modestly decorated room. It had a scarred wooden dresser and two nightstands, a queen sized bed and a small desk. The walls were beige and the ceilings were styled to look like popcorn, like the houses of the 1970s.

Fear sat his briefcase down on the small table beside the window and pulled off his coat and shirt, throwing them aside.

Next, he pulled out his silenced .9mm and sat it down on the dresser beside the bed. Snatching up the remote control; he plopped down in bed and turned on the television. Having found a rerun of Good Times, he sat the remote aside and clasped his hands behind his head. It wasn't long before he found himself drifting off to sleep. An hour had past when he heard someone rapping at the door and disturbing his slumber. Instantly, his eyelids snapped open and he sat up fast, grabbing his .9mm. He chambered a live copper round into the head of his weapon, causing the clinging of metal to resonate throughout the room.

Fear hopped out of bed, boots still on his feet and bullet-proof vest still on his body. Although he slept he made sure to stay on point, being a contract killa he knew that his days on earth were numbered and he'd never let himself be taken out without a fight. Fuck all of that shit. He'd go out letting his gun blaze and bodies fall.

Woof! Woof! Woof! Woof!

Woof! Woof! Woof! Woof!

Fear heard his dogs going crazy behind his motel room's door. He crept to the door cautiously and glanced through the peephole. Through the peephole he saw the clerk at the front desk that had checked him in and given him his key. Tucking his banger at the small of his back, he unchained and unlocked the door. As soon as he pulled it open he came face to face with the nerdy looking Indian clerk, whom adjusted his Coke bottle shaped glasses.

Fear held the door opened to a crack as he addressed the young man. "What's up, family?"

"I forgot to tell you that breakfast is at seven P.M Sharp," he rocked back and forth on his scuffed up high top sneakers, holding firmly to his red vest.

"Good looking out," He tapped his fist to his chest. The clerk gave him a thumb up before walking away.

As soon as Fear shut the door on him and turned around, someone in an all black ninja fit flew into him. The impact to the killa's chest sent him flying back against the door so hard that the large portrait of the forest hanging on the back wall over the bed rattled and fell. The killa shook off his daze and pulled his .9mm from around his back. He went to point it and squeeze off, but the ninja kicked it out of his hand. The weapon went flying across the room, spinning in circles so fast that it looked like a blur. Before Fear could react any further, the intruder was on him like flies on shit. Fists and feet were striking every part of his body that was exposed, even his mothafucking face. When the intruder swung his left fist and then his right fist, the killa caught them and pulled him into him. He wrapped his arms so tightly around him that he winced and squeezed his eyelids shut; feeling like his skeleton was being crushed by an anaconda. The veins of Fear's muscular body bulged all over, etching up his neck and pulsating at his temples. Gritting, he swung the side of his face into the right and left sides of his foe's dome, and then slammed his forehead into his. This caused his foe's eyes to roll all of the way back to their whites and him to moan in pain, his head moving around like a bobble doll. Bringing his hands around the intruder's hips, Fear swiftly swung around to his back and slammed him on his back. The intruder lay there for a moment in agony, but then his eyelids snapped open and he kicked his foe square in the forehead. Fear stumbled backwards and the ninja was left to get to his feet, flipping back upon them. He unsheathed his sword from the center of his back and did several fancy movements with it that the human eye couldn't capture. Once the ninja stopped and raised the katana, he wobbled a little and narrowed his eyelids. Being slammed on his back had weakened him and left him seeing double before his eyes. He went to charge his enemy but stopped himself short, still seeing double. He shook off his daze and looked up, his vision wasn't perfect but he felt like it had focused enough for him to try to finish the fight. In a flash, he charged in swinging the katana up, down and all around, in the form of an X even. With skills formed from years and years of training, Fear dodged the katana with ease. It was like he could see his foe's movements before he'd even thought to make them. One would have thought that he had trained the person trying to kill him. When the intruder found himself with his back to Fear from swinging his blade around so far, he swung it back around and the killa caught his wrist. Fear twisted his wrist and he howled in pain, dropping the sword to the flat carpet. The killa then pulled his enemy's arm behind his back and pulled it up towards his neck, making him holler. He then grabbed him by the back of his head and slammed it hard into the dresser. The impact of the blow stopped all movements from the intruder; he hung limply in Fear's possession, leaving him vulnerable. Seeing that the ninja was at his mercy, the killa yanked the mask from off of his head. His eyelids stretched wide open when he saw who he had in his arms through the reflection of the mirror attached to the dresser. Her head hung at a funny angle and her eyelids flickered white, blood trickling from her left nostril. He studied her face as she moaned in pain, finding it hard to believe that it was her that had tried to take his head.

Taking a deep breath, Fear scooped Eureka into his arms and carried her over to the bed, where he laid her down. Afterwards, he retreated to the bathroom where he folded a washcloth and ran cold water on it. On his way back to the bedroom he heard the telephone ringing. He picked up the receiver as he sat down on the bed, dabbing the blood from Eureka's wounds as she lay still. Her eyes were still to their whites and she was still moaning.

"'Sup?" Fear spoke into the receiver, cradling the telephone to his ear with his shoulder.

"Hey there, buddy. Your neighbors said they heard a lot of loud racket over there, is everything okay?" the clerk asked concerned.

Fear looked to Eureka as he continued to dab her wounds with the washcloth and then answered, "Yeah, everything is okay, homie. I got me a lady friend over here and we got a lil' rough. You know how it is." He cracked a smile.

"Yeah, I know a little something, something about that. Alright, my man. You take it easy. Goodnight." He disconnected the call and Fear hung up right after.

The killa attended to Eureka's wounds until her face was clean of blood. By the time he was done she was fast asleep. Fear sheathed her katana and removed all of the other weapons that she had hidden on her. He placed them all inside of the closet and snatched up a chair en route towards the corner of the room. He picked up his banger from off of the carpet and planted the chair in the corner. Having plopped down, he leaned forward and allowed his gun to dangle between his legs, as he watched a slumbering Eureka. Fear hadn't been asleep in three days. Needless to say, his lack of rest had begun to catch up with him within that hour and he found himself dozing off. His eyelids would narrow and his head would drop. He'd quickly throw it back up and try to shake the fog off of his brain, but eventually, his heavy eyelids won and he found himself asleep.

A short time later Fear's eyelids fluttered open and he looked around woozily, twisting his knuckle at the corner of his eye. His vision was out of focus, but when it finally came into place, he saw that Eureka had vanished from off of the bed. This made the killa look alive. His head snapped to the right of him where he'd propped her katana up against the wall. Swiftly, he reached to his left and found that the weapon had disappeared. Gasping, he whipped around to his right and Eureka pressed the katana to his throat, causing a trickle of blood to fall. Fear's eyelids stretched wide open as his head was tilted back. His pupils were focused on the blade underneath his chin and his lips were partially opened. He dared not to swallow for fear of slicing his own throat. The only thing that he could make out on Eureka was her arms; the rest of her was hidden within the shadows that the room provided. Her knuckles were clutching the katana so tightly that they shown white.

"You make one move and your head is going up towards the ceiling," she swore in a remorseless voice, daring him to fuck up so she could grant his Death Wish.

"G...go ahead...do...do it," His talking that little bit made more blood run down his neck, nearly reaching his collarbone.

"Don't fucking push me!" she spoke with locked jaws, clenching her teeth.

"Nah, you have every right to take my life. Believe you and me, if a nigga had taken my old man's life, I would have been done took his." He spoke the truth. "My ass would be lying at my feet right now in a pool of my own blood, with my throat slit from ear to ear."

There was silence for a few seconds and then he heard her sniffles and whimpers. "I know you'd do it, but what if it was me that had done it." Hurriedly, she took one hand off of the kilt to wipe her tearing eyes with the back of her fist.

Fear shut his eyelids briefly and took a deep breath, before responding, "I...I wouldn't...if it was you."

Eureka took the katana away from his throat, and with a grunt, she spun around and kicked him in the back of the neck. His head snapped forward and he hit the carpet, landing on his palms. He whipped his head around and caught a foot in the jaw, sending specks of blood flying everywhere. The killa fell on his back and she straddled him, grasping his neck. He lay still allowing her to choke him, his eyes turning glassy and bulging. Veins bulged at his temples and neck, the color of his face turning Smurf blue. He balled his fists tightly showcasing all of the veins they were riddled with. His eyes stared up at the ceiling and bled tears down his cheek, as his tongue hung slightly out of his mouth. Wrinkled appeared at the corners of her eyes and she gritted, sobbing. Her eyes were focused down at his face, as she applied more pressure to his neck. At the moment she loved and hated him. She wanted him dead, but yet she wanted him alive. Inside of her head she was so confused. Here was the man that had murdered her father in cold blood, and she wanted to be in his arms forever and ever. She was disgusted with herself for wanting to do anything other than kill him. No one could tell her that her Bootsy wasn't turning over in his grave seeing his daughter. She saw herself as a traitor, nothing more, and nothing less. How could she look at herself any other way? Although she be-lieved that it was all true, she couldn't help how she felt about the man that lay at mercy. If she could have done it all over again, she would have never reached out for his help when she and her brother caught that beef with Malvo. Hell naw, she would have taken her chances out in the street and dealt with that bitch ass nigga when the time came. But now it was too late, she had play the hands that she was dealt.

"Grrrrr," Eureka threw her head back and looked up at the ceiling, keeping her hands around Fear's neck. Suddenly, she threw her head down and found herself looking into his eyes, dripping teardrops into his face. The droplets splashed against the lower half of his face, "God damn youuuuuu! God damn you to hell..." she took the time to whimper, swallowing her spit and continuing on, " and God damn me...for still being in love with the man that murdered my faaatheerrr." She shuddered hard and squeezed her eyelids shut, loosening her grip around his throat. She fell on top of him, sobbing long and hard, while he gasped for air and blinked his eyelids rapidly. Once he gathered his wits and regulated his breath-ing, his arms slowly snaked around her small form and embraced it against his own.

"How...how did you find me?" he asked hoarsely.

"Our cell phones...the GPS's in them."

"Right," *He responded, wondering how he could have forgotten it.*

For a while they laid there on the floor listening to one another's breathing and feeling each other's chest with the beating of their hearts. Eureka's head rose from off of Fear's chest and she looked up into his eyes. There weren't any words between them for a moment, but then, she inched towards him and mashed her lips against his own. Her lips peeled apart and she stuck her tongue inside of his mouth, turning her head as she kissed him long, deep and hard. He reciprocated this action, and their lips smacking resonated through the room. It wasn't long before she was nibbling and sucking on his neck, her hands busy unbuckling his thick leather belt, the metal of the buckle clinking as she unfastened it. She pulled the belt loose and threw it aside, unzipping his jeans and pulling his meat free from his denim prison. She pulled her glove from off of her small hand and let it drop off to the side. She then spit in her palm and reached back, using her saliva to lubricate his love muscle. It grew long and strong, pulsating at the head. His thick shaft had veins running up and down it. A clear liquid ran from out of the hole of his penis, manhood jumping he was so horny. Eureka lifted herself off of him and quickly pulled off her pants. With one strong tug, he yanked her thong free of her meaty buttocks and left shreds of the fabric lying on the floor. He went to grab her by her hips, but she interlocked her fingers with his and forced his hands back against the surface, pinning them down. Carefully, she lowered her butt towards the head of his member, until it was at the front of the entrance of her slickened pink hole. He narrowed his eyelids and licked his lips, feeling the high temperature of her pussy. He couldn't wait to meet that snug fit of hers. Before he knew it, he was gasping feeling himself filling up that void between her thick thighs.

Eureka's eyes rolled to the back of her head and she breathed loud and hard. His dick felt so good and she couldn't get enough of it. She couldn't help but think that it was this dick that had driven that bitch Constance crazy.

"Uh! Uh! Uh! Uh!" Eureka slammed herself up and down on that dick, pussy making sloshing noises.

Fear's pupils rolled into the back of his head and he clenched her meaty ass cheeks, hands sinking into her buttocks. A white lather built up on his thick, veined dick and he began to moan, which turned Eureka on. Hearing him enjoying himself, she started to speed up and his toes curled up inside of his boots. He licked his lips and bit down on his bottom one, forcing his head back. She took his hands and placed them on her succulent breasts, clenching them a little so that he'd be holding them firmly. She leaned back on him and planted her hands on his thighs, moving her hips like a belly dancer. This caused him to moan louder and turned her on further. She looked down at his face and frowned, moving her hips that much faster. Before long this had him moaning and groaning like a little bitch. She smiled devilishly. This was because she was used to being the vulnerable one, and now he was the one wearing those shoes.

"Ahhhh, shiiiiit!" Fear's nostrils flared and his eyelids fluttered.

"Unh huh, that's right, this my dick!" Eureka said, beads of sweat oozing out of her forehead, sliding down her face.

"Ooooh, fuck!" he turned his head from side to side, feeling his throbbing penis build up with semen.

"Who dick is this? Huh? Who this dick belong to?" Eureka asked, hot and sweaty, wetness sliding down her body.

"Eu...Eu...Eu..." he stuttered the pussy was so good.

"Unh huh, tell me, daddy, tell me, who this dick belong to," Sweat trickled from her brows and she went faster, dripping her wetness on him.

"Eu...Eu...Euuuureeeeekaaaaaaa!" Fear clenched her breasts so hard that redness formed around his fingers and he slammed his hardness deeper inside of her, busting hard and long inside of her. He frowned and veins bulged all over his face and body. He clenched his teeth so tight that it felt like they were going to break. Her face twisted into a mask of pleasure and she came to. Her hot liquid came down, soiling his hairy nut sack. Spent, with him still inside of her, she lay down on top of him and kissed his lips. Afterwards, she pressed the side of her face against his chest and he wrapped his strong, vein riddled arms around her. He kissed the top of her head and they both shut their eyes. Their hot, sticky bodies became one. They listened to one another's heart beats as they drifted off to sleep.

The next morning

Frowning, Fear's eyelids fluttered open and he looked around. He went to wrap his arms tighter around Eureka and that's when he noticed that she was gone. Instantly, he sat up and looked around, thin rays of sunlight shining on his face from in between the blinds. He wiped out the little bit of scum that was at the corners of his eyes and got to his feet, pushing himself up from off the floor with the assistance of the nightstand beside the bed. Looking at the bed, he found a message written on the pillow with an ink pen. Hurriedly, he snatched up the pillow and read over it, lines etching across his forehead.

Due to the circumstances, we can't be together in this life, but there's always the next. Until then, consider this my goodbye...forever.

Love for all of eternity,

Eureka

Fear tossed the pillow aside and took a deep breath. Turning around, he rubbed his hand down his waves. When he looked up, he saw Eureka's thong hanging off of the lamp shade. Quickly, he snatched up the thong and held it to his nose with both hands. Shutting his eyelids, he took a deep breath and inhaled Eureka's womanly scent. He held the pose that he was in for a time before taking the thong from his nose and stuffing it into his back pocket. Afterwards, he looked out through the blinds and saw his Rottweilers where he'd left them.

***

As soon as Fear walked out of his motel room he spotted his Rottweilers and lines creased his forehead. Walking towards them, he narrowed his eyelids seeing something sticking out of their backs. When he was upon them, the beasts went crazy barking and jumping up on him. Kneeling down, he held each one of them against him and pulled out what he had seen sticking up out of them from a far. They were tranquilizer darts. He was sure that they had been laced with a sedative. A smirk creased his lips realizing that he had taught Eureka well, little momma had taken out the hounds and then moved in to finish him off. Acknowledging this made him very proud.

"I don't know what I'm gonna do with you guys, but I've gotta think of something 'cause I can't take you with me where I'm going." Fear told the Rottweilers, like they could under-stand what he was saying. They were staring up at him panting with their wet tongues hanging out of the side of their mouths.

Fear threw the tranquilizer darts aside and played with the hounds for a second. He then untied them from the bumper of his vehicle. He was about to place them into the backseat when the sound of drumming from across the parking lot drew his attention. He looked over in the direction that the noise was coming from and found a blind man beating on the bottoms of white mop buckets, making unique music. The old man flipped the drumsticks over in his palms and kept right along beating and nodding his head. Fear looked from the blind man playing the street drums to his Rottweilers, whom were nodding their heads to the beat. This brought a smile to *his face. Tugging on the twin leashes, he brought the beasts along. They strolled beside him, wagging their tails and panting. Fear stopped at the left of the old man as he continued to create the street music. Once he was done, he flipped the sticks over his back and caught them, rising to his feet and taking a bow. Still smiling and holding the leashes, the killa applauded the old man's performance.*

"Bravo, bravo, bravo." Fear continued to clap. "Man, youz a bad mothafucka on them drums."

"Thank you, thank you, thank you," The old man took off his hat and gave him a nod, before smacking it back on his head.

"I'm Al. What's yo' name?" The killa extended his hand right by his face.

"Well, I'm Bernie...Bernie Gladstone," The old man shook his hand firmly. The old blind man was about seventy years old. He was a hefty fellow with a double chin, covered in white stubble. He sported a porkpie hat and a plaid shirt underneath a tattered black blazer. The black shades that covered his eyes were as dark as the tinted windows on a limousine.

"Cool. Check this out, OG, I'ma be leaving town pretty soon and where I'm going ain't animal friendly." He lied. "I thought that maybe you'd like to have my boys. You know, I was thinking that you could use them like a couple of Seeing Eye dogs or something." He held out the leashes toward him.

"You sure, youngin?" Bernie asked in his signature gravelly voice, looking in the direction that he heard the voice coming from.

"Positive." He took his meaty hand and placed the leashes into his palm, closing it.

"Thank you, son," He smiled gratefully, rising to his feet slowly and opened his arms for an embrace. Smiling, Fear hugged the old gent and stashed a bank-roll of money inside of

his blazer's pocket. He patted him on the back, continuing to smile as he bid him a farewell.

"You take it easy, alright?" The old man nodded and Fear kneeled down to the twin Rottweilers. He rubbed and massaged the beasts behind their ears as they licked his face, leaving shiny streaks behind on his jovial face. "You guys take care of your new master for me, okay?" the dogs barked up at their former master. "Alright then, I'm gonna miss you niggaz, family." He kissed both of the dogs and patted Bernie's shoulder as he strolled past him, hopping inside of his vehicle and driving off. The killa left dust in his wake as he sped off down the road.

The Rottweilers barked at the back of their master's ride while Bernie waved goodbye to it. Feeling something inside of his pocket, he dipped his hand inside of his blazer's pocket and pulled out the bank-roll that Fear had stashed there. Instantly, tears slid down his cheeks and dripped off of his chin. He looked up and continued to stare in the direction that he believed that the killa had driven off in, waving.

"I've never met a kinder, passionate, gentler man in my entire life." Bernie claimed. "God bless you, young blood. God bless you."

Bernie stacked his buckets inside of one another and sat them inside of the shopping cart he had hidden out of sight. After dropping the drumsticks into the space of the area were a customer would sit their child inside of the shopping cart, he tied the leashes of the Rottweilers to the handle of the shopping cart and walked off, whistling. His plan was to get himself something hot to eat and set up shop at his next location to hustle himself up some more money. Bernie walked off into the rising sun, him and his hounds looking like silhouettes as they walked along.

The night before, Fear and Eureka made love for what they believed would be the very last time and conceived a boy she would go on to name, Kingston.

Present

Ain't this about a bitch, nigga is my nephew's father, Anton thought. *Sis got skeletons in her closet that I don't even know about.*

Anton's face softened and then he scowled, nose scrunching up. "Fuck that shit! This nigga ain't getting no passes." He went to finish Fear off with his Eagle's Claw, but then he remembered something.

Oh shit! Raymar's getting away, that's a million dollar bag, the baby face killa thought and looked up the road, seeing the speeding Honda that Raymar had made his escape in. Acknowledging this, he dropped his hand to his side and looked down at the man that was at his mercy. "This shit ain't over, homeboy, we gone settle this shit up later." He swore to Fear, kicking him in his side and causing him to howl out in pain.

Anton took off running back to his motorcycle. Hopping back on it, he revved that bitch up and took off down the street, leaving tire prints on the black top and smoke wafting in the air.

Eureka sniffled and wiped her dripping eyes with the back of her hand. She then took a deep breath and headed in Fear's direction. Reaching him, she got him upon his feet with his assistance and threw his arm over her shoulders, making their way back towards her Chevy Impala.

"My…my son, huh?" Fear managed to say in pain.

"Yeah…your son," Eureka replied, helping him into the backseat of the Impala and slamming the door shut behind him. She then ran over to the driver's door and hopped inside behind the wheel, firing up the engine and busting a U-turn. Next, she sped off back in the direction that she'd came.

Ain't love grand?

Chapter Two

Boom! Boom! Boom! Boom!

The double doors of the mansion rattled and resonated as a powerful force attempted to get inside. Tristan, heart beating, palms sweaty approached the door. He had the stock of his shotgun braced against his shoulder and the business end of his weapon leveled at the mansion's entrance. His heart pounded inside of his rib cage and bumped up against his chest bone. He didn't know what the fuck was on the other side of those doors, but when it came before his eyes he was going to blow its mothafucking head clean off.

Ba-Boom!

The double doors flew inward and Tristan found a white man clad in body armor and wearing a holster strapped to his thigh that contained a Desert Eagle. Wearing a neoprene mask on the lower half of his face and having a form ripe for summer made him look like an action figure or some super hero from a Saturday morning cartoon. Tristan glanced over the man's shoulder and found a late model Cadillac Seville parked on the lawn. There were tire prints on the pretty green grass and in the background one of the gates was hanging off of its hinges. It came to mind then that the hit-man must have had some sort of gadget to disrupt all electrical devices which was why every electronic device had stopped working inside of the house. This had allowed him access on the estates grounds without being detected.

For a time the men stood where they were mad dogging one another, their chests rising and dropping with every breath that they took. Having grown tired of the stare down, Julian made the first move and that's when Tristan's shotgun roared to life. The impact from the blast lifted the hit-man off of his booted feet and sent him skidding across the porch. Tristan stood there for a time with his shotgun smoking. He waited for the man to get back up, but he never did. Figuring that he'd killed him off, he cautiously moved in on him. He kept his eyes on him and his trigger finger on the ready. Tristan got within three feet of his victim before he kicked him twice to see if he would budge. When he didn't, he sighed with relief feeling that his reign of terror was over. Suddenly, Julian's eyelids snapped open and he peeled his lips apart. Something shiny and silver was clenched between his teeth twinkling. He spat it out and three poisonous needles stabbed into his attacker's neck. He winced and staggered back surprised. He threw up the hand that held the shotgun and it blasted off into the sky. Tristan spun around and fell to the ground. He blinked his eyelids uncontrollably and pulled the needles out of his neck. When he looked at them they had blood at the tips of them. Tossing them aside, he scrambled onto his feet and staggered towards the mansion. His blurry vision came in and out of focus as he looked over his shoulder to see if Julian was on his ass, which he was. The hit-man was strolling casually in his direction as if he didn't have a care in the world, whistling Dixie.

"Oh fuck!" His eyes widen seeing that the killa was closing in on him. He nearly fell on his way up the steps, but quickly regained his equilibrium. Crossing the threshold into the mansion, he whipped around with his fists up ready to get active with the perp. "Come on, big boy! Come get these hands!"

Seeing the assassin pull his bow-gun from off his back, Tristan's eyelids shot open and he made off of the porch quickly. He ran as fast as he could, breathing heavily and hoping that he didn't catch one in his back.

"Haa! Haa! Haa! Haa!" he huffed and puffed while hauling ass. He glanced over his shoulder and he saw the hit-man pointing the bowgun at him. He made to zig-zag and that's when he heard the arrow whizzing through the air. The sound of it zeroing in on his eardrums as it drew closer. Before he knew it he felt something sharp pierce his back and send him hurtling towards the living room wall. He screamed at the top of his lungs as he flew across the room, slamming into the wall. The impact caused him to wince and the portrait he, Eureka and Kingston to rattle where it hung. The portrait rocked back and forth before falling to the floor and cracking down its middle.

Tristan hollered and screamed trying to push himself off of the wall, but there wasn't any use. He was stuck to the wall like a nail that had been hammered to it. The area of his body that had been punctured by the arrow was quickly being absorbed by blood. He turned and twisted as he gritted trying his damndest to pull himself free. Grabbing the end of the arrow he tried to pull it out and break it off but he wasn't strong enough. Doing this only succeeded in him causing blood to run down the length of the projectile and slick his fingers wet.

Suddenly, Julian grabbed a handful of Tristan's curly hair and pulled his head back. When he did this his victim's eyelids turned into slits and he squared his jaws, showcasing the muscles in them.

"Grrrrrrr." he growled like a lion disturbed from its slumber.

"Where is Fear?" Julian asked really slowly. His face was stern and unforgiving.

"Who?" he asked through gritted teeth.

"Fear."

"Oh, Fear. Hold on, let me pull 'em outta my ass. Hahahahaha!" having his head slammed into the wall split his forehead open and a slither of blood ran. His eyes rolled to their whites and his head lulled about. He was barely conscious and moaning.

Julian pulled his head back by his hair again. "Is anyone else here?"

"I'm not...I'm not telling you jack, shit-head!" he gritted.

"Is dat right?"

"Fucking aye." he croaked in pain.

"I'm gonna take it dat neither he, nor Eureka are here. Fine, I guess I'll settle for the boy instead."

"What...what boy?"

"This boy." he pulled out a picture of Kingston and brought it before his eyes.

"That's...that's...my...my...son."

"Hmmm, interesting." the killa raised an eyebrow. "Where is he?"

Seeing something flying by at the corner of his eye, Julian's head snapped in its direction. He dropped the picture and drew his knife, throwing it with all of his might. It spiraled in circles heading towards it mark. The blade buried halfway inside of the maid, Alice's, shoulder. She hit the floor hard balling up her face as she felt the pain soaring throughout her shoulder. Taking his time, Julian stashed his bow-gun on his back and made his way toward her. Standing over her, he dropped the picture of Kingston near her face where she could see it.

"Where is this child?" He asked, mashing the heel of his shoe down on the kilt of the knife in her shoulder, causing her to release a scream intense enough to burst eardrums.

She rasped out of breath as she attempted to answer him. "I don't...I don't...I don't know."

"Wrong answer," He mashed his foot down further against the kilt, pushing the blade deeper into her flesh and making blood flow in a river.

"Arghhhhh," She screamed aloud, showcasing all of the teeth and pinkness inside of her mouth. Tears oozed out of her narrowed eyes and encircled her face as she dug her fingers into the carpeted floor. He let his foot up off of the kilt and relieved some of her pain. She hung her head and her shoulders hunched up and down as she breathed huskily. She didn't have an idea where Tristan had stashed Kingston because she was trying to find somewhere to hide as soon as she knew some shit was about to pop off.

"Tell me where I can locate da boy, or I shall bring you to ya demise, woman." He snatched the Desert Eagle from out of the holster strapped to his thigh, holding it at his side inside of his leather gloved hand. He pressed his boot down against the center of her back, pinning her down to the surface. For a second he listened to her moaning and groaning before growing agitated with her response, or lack thereof. "Tell me, tell me now gotdamn it 'fore I put a bullet in da back of ya bloody skull."

Bringing her head back up she shouted, "Go to hell!"

"You fust, bitch!"

Blam!

The first shot blew half of her head apart, sending brain fragments and red pieces of skull everywhere. Specs of blood speckled the side of the white couch. He leveled his head bussa at her back and gritted, dumping on her and watching her corpse twitch, like it was going through convulsions. When he was finished he tucked his smoldering weapon back inside of its holster and pulled the tranquilizer gun from the holster at the small of his back. He pulled a dart from the row of them lining the belt that was strapped around his opposite thigh. After he loaded one into the weapon, he went about the hunt for young Kingston, whistling Dixie as he climbed the stairs. He gently pushed opened door after door, peeking his head inside of each bedroom. Once he found the one that resembled a child's, he made his way inside.

Kingston was still in the back of his parents' closet staring out through the shudder door. The reflection of the outside light shone in on his face. All he could hear was his own heavy breathing as he watched Julian walk back and forth across the bedroom, lifting and turning over shit, looking for his little ass. Abruptly, he stopped at the center of the floor in the path of the closet causing Kingston to hold his breath. His tiny heart was beating so fast that his shirt twitched with its every thump. The hit-man did a slow counter clockwise spin were he stood until he was facing the closet and had locked eyes with the little boy. The youth's eyes bugged and he gasped, stepping back away from the door. He bumped up against the wall, but then his face transformed into a scowl when he remembered when his uncle Anton told him to fear nothing and no one. With that in mind, he clenched his small fists and got into a martial arts fighting stance.

Julian smiled like the cat that had swallowed the canary when he realized his prey was hiding inside of the closet. He licked his lips and started for the door.

"Why there ya are, ya lil' fella," as soon as he turned the knob and opened the door, a battle cry shook his ear drums and Kingston came running at him full speed ahead. The assassin's eyes widen and his mouth hung open. "What the fu...Ooof!" A sharp kick doubled him over causing him to drop the tranquilizer gun and cupped his balls. He went cross eyed and groaning, squaring his jaws. The little dude round house kicked him across the jaw which sent him falling up against the side of the bed wincing. "Ahhhh," Seeing that his predator was out of commission, Kingston took the advantage and hauled ass out of the bedroom, sights set on the staircase. Julian bit down on his bottom lip to combat the pain in his lower region as he scrambled around on his knees, searching for the dart shooting weapon. When he zeroed in on it, a wicked smile stretched across his lips. He grabbed it up and took a stance on his knee, extending his weapon and shutting one eye to take aim. He stuck his tongue out of the corner of his mouth, as he waited for the right time to fire. "Run Forest, run," The hit man spoke in a soft tone, watching the youth run for his life.

"Haa! Haa! Haa! Haa," Kingston ran as fast as he could, huffing and puffing. His heart was beating with a vendetta behind his chest and he hoped he wouldn't be shot. Please, God, don't let 'em kill me, he thought as his made tracks like he was in a marathon, eyes shut, adrenaline pumping like mad through his body.

"Got 'em." Julian spoke to no one in particular as he held his weapon outstretched. His target was almost at the staircase when his finger curled around the trigger.

Pewk!

The dart whistled through the air like an arrow en route to its intended mark.

Haa! Haa! Haa! Haa! Haa!

Kingston bowed his head and squeezed his eyelids tighter, running even faster.

Shhhhhhhhhhh!

The dart whistled through the air looking like a blur while in motion.

Haa! Haa! Haa! Haa! Haa!

Kingston couldn't see it but he could feel its deadly aura around him so he ran that much faster.

Shhhhhhhhhhh!

The dart was twisting around headed in the direction of the youth.

Julian smiled harder looking like a sneaky rodent about the face.

"Dat's ya ass." He just knew he'd gotten him.

Thwack!

His eyes went big and he mouthed 'What the fuck' when the dart stabbed into the wall. It missed his prey by a mere inch as he made a left, hurrying down the staircase.

How in da hell did I miss? Julian couldn't help thinking.

"Son of a bitch," The hit-man rose to his feet, pissed off that he'd missed his target. He pulled another dart from the Velcro strap around his thigh and loaded it up, cocking it back. He held his aching balls with one hand as he hurriedly limped along while the other held tight to his tranquilizer gun. Heading down the corridor, he looked over the guard railing to see Kingston half way down the staircase, "Where do you think ya going, ya brat? Huh?" The assassin made it to the top of the steps just in time to see the youngster reaching the first floor.

Kingston was on his way out of the door when something at the corner of his eye stole his attention.

"Dad?" he frowned up seeing his father impaled to the wall. He made to go help him but his father's yelling froze him in place.

"Get outta here, son, go!" Tristan yelled at him, looking very weak and exhausted from where he was stuck against the wall.

"But dad…" his eyes misted with tears and his bottom lip quivered.

"Please, son, hurry," His pleading eyes urging him to get the hell out of there, "Hurry, run for your life!"

Kingston's eyes lingered on his father for a time longer, his chest swelling and falling with each breath. Abruptly, he took off running out of the house, nearly being hit by the poisonous dart that Julian had launched at him from the top step. The dart stabbed into the door just as Kingston cleared the threshold on his way out. He hurried down the steps making tracks across the lawn. Just then, the UK hit-man made it out on the front porch, watching the youngster's back as he ran off, occasionally looking over his shoulder.

Julian lifted his tranquilizer gun and took aim, pulling the trigger. The weapon jerked when it unleashed another tainted dart. It whizzed through the air, seemingly slowly rotating while on course to its target's back.

The impact of the tranquilizer dart caused Kingston to stumble forward and crash to the lawn. He lay there wincing and beginning stages of passing out. He pushed up from the ground on wobbly arms. He went to stand to his feet and fell flat on his face. Shutting his eyelids, he took one deep breath and his shoulders fell. The rest of his breaths were calm and steady. A shadow came from behind and eclipsed his body where it lay limp. Julian pressed his boot against the little nigga'z back, grabbed a hold of the dart and yanked that bitch out. Next, he pulled two pairs of zip-cuffs out and laid one on his back. He used the first pair to cuff his wrists behind his back and the second pair to secure his ankles. Afterwards, he tossed his little ass over his shoulder and carried him off to the rear of his Cadillac. He dumped him inside. Standing over Kingston while he held open the trunk, he observed him for a moment before slamming it shut. He smacked imaginary dust off of his hands and glanced back at the mansion where he saw Tristan continue to struggle to get off of the wall that he was pinned against.

Julian made his way around his Cadillac and jumped in behind the wheel. He cranked that big bastard up and went on about his business whistling Dixie.

***

In the back of a pool hall a meeting between some of the most dangerous criminal outfits in Rio was taking place underneath everyone's noses. The men present were the head niggaz in charge of some of the fiercest gangs in the beautiful city. As of now they were taking swigs of Coronas and chopping up hood politics.

"So, Fearless is gone, huh? You think he's ever coming back?" Gold Mouth's bald head ass asked, folding his enormous arms across his chest. He was a big, tall son of a bitch with a head like a goddamn Rottweiler.

"I don't know, but without him Nero is weak." Lupe stated. He was a short fellow with a flat top styled haircut and a thin mustache. His scrawny ass was in a wife beater which he wore beneath an ugly ass red shirt, with palm trees scattered on it.

"Weak? Fearless is one fuckin' man, Nero has an entire army." Gold Mouth looked at him like he didn't know what the fuck he was talking about.

29

"Naaah," Raphael shook his head. He was a slender dude with a muscular physique. His head was shaved on the sides and his hair was braided into two cornrows. "Without Fearless the rest of those cats are lil' more denna couple of punks with guns, ya feel me? I say we take 'em." He looked around at the rest of the niggaz there, coming into eye contact with all of them.

"I agree. I say we move on Nero," Keno spoke on the situation at hand. He was a dark skinned cat that rocked a thick ass beard and an eye patch over his left eye, which also had a jagged scar running down it. "He got soldiers and we got soldiers. He got guns and we got guns."

"Right, but he has a lil' more of both than us," Raphael reminded him.

"Not that much more. If we take it to 'em, we'll have a fighting chance." He looked him square in his eyes.

"How'd you figga that?" Lupe asked.

"Think about it. With all of us combined, we'll be virtually unstoppable." He looked around at all of the men surrounding him.

"Hmmmm, you may have a point." Gold Mouth massaged his stubble riddled chin. He began pacing the floor as he thought things over. The rest of the men exchanged glances and focused on him, watching him with curious eyes.

"What's on yo' mind, G?" Keno asked, a line creasing his forehead.

Suddenly, Gold Mouth stopped dead in his tracks, holding his wrists at his back, head bowed. The expression he wore across his face told everyone present that he was still thinking about something. He lifted his head and looked around at everyone before taking his time to speak.

"You're right, Keno. With the combined efforts of our men getting Nero's people out of the way shouldn't be a problem at all. Once the war is over we'll hold stake to our piece of the slums without having to kick up any taxes to the powers that be. We should also agree to stay on our own side of the fence; no matter what lick may garner our attention on the other side. I'm sure you all remember, like it was before Nero rose to power?" the leaders nodded their understanding. "Good. Then it's settled."

"How do you propose we get our soldiers to go along with this partnership?" Lupe inquired, brows raised,

"Although we're all enemies and we've managed to let cooler heads prevail, that doesn't mean our guys will."

"They will. You sell 'em a dream of having their piece of the slums to themselves again and not having to kick fifty percent up to Nero. That will be more than enough. Trust me. No real man wants to have to bend to the will of another." The rest of the leaders nodded in agreement of his statement.

"Alright then, it's settled. We put out the word to our guys and prepare them to move on Nero in three days. That should give us enough time to come up with a plan and a strategy." Lupe looked around at all of the leaders. They nodded their approval.

After the meeting, the criminals shook hands and left in their respective vehicles. Unbeknownst to them they had a traitor among them that was going to tell their enemy their little secret.

***

Kingston lay in the trunk of Julian's Cadillac bumping around with each dip and pothole the vehicle met. Slowly, his eyelids fluttered open and he found himself staring at the red brake lights of the car. He was in darkness save for the outside light that shone through the cracks and crevasses of the vehicle. He tried to move his arm and ankles and found that they were bound. When he went to scream he discovered that his lips were sealed shut by the tape stretched over them. He struggled to get himself lose and found that the more he did so the hotter it became and the harder it was for him to breathe. Establishing this in his young mind, he figured that it was best for him to lie still until he could think of some other way to get free.

Kingston's face scrunched up and he shut his eyelids, tears bursting through them. He whimpered and his body shuddered uncontrollably. For as brave as he was he was still just a child.

Please, dad, save me, he thought, pleeeease.

Meanwhile

Tristan gritted and threw his head back. His crimson stained hand clenched the end of the arrow that had him pinned to the wall while he was trying to push off of the wall, foot pressed against it. More blood traveled down the length of the arrow's shaft and dripped on the floor. His face balled tightly and veins came up his neck and arms, as he strained himself trying to get free to rescue his son.

"I'm coming, son, I'm comiiing," he called out. "Daddy's coming…For you. Grrrrr."

Little by little the arrow began to slide out from where it was embedded inside of the wall.

Chapter Three

Anton's motorcycle flew up the road closing the distance between its self and the Honda that Raymar was in, quickly. The panicking Brazilian fugitive looked back and forth between the windshield and over his shoulder at the young hitta. He didn't know what the young man had in mind to do to him and he wasn't going to let him catch him to find out. In a flash, Raymar popped open the glove box and loose paperwork and napkins came spilling out onto the floor, along with a Glock .40. The gun landed on its nose and fell on its side, sitting upon some of the documents. Raymar kept his eyes on the road and hurriedly felt for the weapon, coming across some of the papers that had fallen out. As soon as he felt the plastic handle of the banger, he shot back up in his seat and pointed it out of the window. Pulling the trigger in succession, his hand slightly jerked with each copper headed round that it spat.

Anton popped a Willie on his motorcycle and sped towards the fugitive, sparks deflecting off of the bottom of his bike. Using his weight, Anton brought his motorcycle back down and ripped up the road en route towards the Honda that housed the man of his desire. Swiftly, he pulled the pistol-grip Mausberg pump from out of the holster on his bike and pointed it, just as Raymar was about to take another shot at him.

Bloom!

The blast from the deadly weapon shattered the back window of the Honda. The hot pellets sizzled against the back of Raymar's neck causing him to grimace and duck, squeezing his eyelids shut. He gritted hard, and when he peeled his eyelids back open his eyes were glassy. Getting a tighter grip on his compact handgun, he went to take another shot at

Anton, but the reoccurring blasts from the pump made him think again. Anton blew off the side view mirror so Raymar wouldn't be able to see him to take another shot at him. The young hitta then targeted the back tires and blew them to shreds, causing the snitch to lose control of the vehicle. The tricked out Honda fishtailed and its driver struggled to gain control of it. He dropped his Glock on the floor and cursed aloud. Right when he'd gained control of the car, his pursuer appeared on the side of him and blew out his front driver side tire. It sounded like a small explosion with the pump's pellets met the black rubber tire, sending it swerving out of control. Again, Raymar tried to regain control of the vehicle, but it was already too late, that mothafucka had flipped over. Landing on its rooftop, the Honda slid a yard down the road. Raymar shook off his daze as he hung upside down, looking to his left and seeing Anton on his motorcycle speeding towards him. The young hitta holstered his smoking pistol-grip shotgun on the side of his bike and sped up towards his latest target with a vendetta.

"Oh shit," Raymar's eyes nearly popped out of his fucking head seeing Anton headed in his direction. He hurriedly tried to unbuckle his safety belt, but the goddamn thing wouldn't come un-done. He breathed huskily and looked back and forth between the task at hand and the young hitta heading for him. He seemed to be getting closer and closer by the second. This made the Brazilian's heart beat harder and faster inside of his chest. No matter how hard the poor bastard tried, he couldn't unbuckle the safety belt. Before he knew it Anton was coming to a stop alongside the Honda and placing the kick-stand down. Raymar knew that he was fucked now. "Fuck, fuck, fuuuuck!" he repeatedly slammed his fist into the ceiling of the vehicle, hating himself for not being able to get away. Seeing Anton reaching to open the driver side door, he decided to cop a plea for his life. "Please, man, please, don't kill me!" he said with his hands together begging. Suddenly, the door was thrown open and sunlight shined in on the upper half of Raymar, which was in the shadowed area of the vehicle. With tears on the verge of running from his eyes, the Brazilian fugitive narrowed his eyelids against the illumination of the sun and tried to get a look at the young hitta's face. He could only see him from the chest on down being that the sun was shining on his back, leaving the rest of him in the shade.

"Please, don't kill me, man, don't kill me, I'm begging you." Raymar whimpered like the bitch made ass nigga that he was, seeing the youth pull a bowie knife from where it was sheathed on his thigh. The sun kissed off of the blade and a rainbow was born. Raymar squeezed his eyelids shut and trembled all over, hands still together begging for his pathetic ass life. Anton kneeled down and used the knife to slice the restraints that were the safety belt from the foreigner's form. This action caused Raymar to fall to the ceiling of the wrecked vehicle, wincing. Before he could make a move, he was being pulled out of the Honda by his ankle and shoved up against the vehicle. A scowling Anton sheathed his blade and beat the shit out of him. He gave him body shots and face shots that opened up wounds on his face and bruised him badly. When Raymar went to double over, he chopped him in his throat and made him gag. His eyes lit up and he grabbed his neck with both hands. His thoughts were taken off the stinging in his throat when the youth kicked the side of his leg outward. The impact made a sickening noise that sounded like a chicken bone snapping in two and he fell to his left, propped up on one bending knee. Throwing his head back, he hollered so loud that Anton was positive that God and all of his angels heard him.

"That'll guarantee that cho punk ass won't be running anywhere anytime soon." Anton cracked him in the chin and knocked him out cold. He fell to the warm ground on the side of his face, cheek mashed up against it. He snored hard and loud.

Seeing that his target was unconscious, Anton took in the full scope of his surroundings. Not too far away he saw a modest looking white house with a Toyota pickup truck in its driveway. A smile emerged on his lips when he seen it. This was because Raymar was a fugitive and he knew the law would be looking for him. With the truck he could transport his motorcycle and use it to keep his capture's identity concealed.

With that thought in mind, Anton woke Raymar's bitch ass up and made him get to his feet at gunpoint. He climbed back upon his motorcycle and cranked that bad boy up. Still holding his weapon on the Brazilian fugitive, he made him mount the back of his bike and wrap his arms around him. Next, he holstered his banger and threatened to kill him if he tried anything on their way to their destination.

***

Eureka looked back and forth between the windshield and the rearview mirror at Fear. He was bloody and swollen, looking like he went a few rounds with a young Iron Mike Tyson. His pupils rolled up in the back of his head, displaying his milky white eyes. His lips were busted and his nose was twice its size. Eureka cringed inside. Anton had done a real number on him, but she knew that he'd let him beat the dog shit out of him. Fear was a better fighter than her little brother. She was sure he could have taken him out, but it was his love for her and her brother that stopped him from killing him.

"How you doing back there, champ?" she asked, slightly adjusting the rearview mirror.

"Ugh, anyone get the license plate of that truck?" Fear moaned.

"Yeah, it read Anton." She cracked a grin and he laughed, sounding a little muffled.

"I could tell that he'd been training for this moment since I left Killa Cali."

"He has training, training very intensely," her face suddenly turned serious.

Flashback

The sun seemed to be beaming its brightest that evening. Its rays shined through the partially cloudy sky and warmed the backs of the men below. There were seven of them in all, but one of them stood out like a fly in butter milk. This nigga was naked from the neck down and dressed in a pair of black parachute pants. He had a fighter's physique. His body was well defined by muscle and veins. The nasty scars that had amassed over his torso over time gave him character, and told the horrors of some of his most fierce battles and near death experiences. The expression he wore was one of concentration and determination. He stood in a martial arts fighting stance, his eyes bouncing around to all of the hard faces of the men in his presence.

They surrounded him, all seven of them. His front, his back, his sides; he was trapped in the center of them. He was ready though. He was born ready. Shit, he was born to kill, that's how he made his living. So this was nothing more than child's play for him. Fists before his eyes, his head snapped in every which direction. His keen eyes taking in the hostile looks of the white garbed, black belts that encircled him, poised to take his fucking head off. They had a katana, dagger, kon, nun chucks, guillotine and saitachis. The men were all still like they were frozen. They were watching him closely and he was watching them. They wanted blood and he wanted their lives. All of their lives.

A bird screeched as it soared high across the sky, setting shit off.

"Ahhhh!" the assailant hollered as he charged forth with his kon. "Ooof!" a kick to the midsection sent his ass back where he came. He hit the ground hard as a mothafucka on his back and rolled back, tumbling.

Wop! Wap! Crack! Anton's fists and bare feet were like blurs in motion. He moved so fucking fast that these niggaz didn't even know that he'd budged. All he saw was that nigga that had murdered his father's face before his maddening eyes. The assault that he dished out gave his opponents expressions of agony and this brought him great satisfaction. But it was only because he imagined that each and every one of them were his arch nemesis, Fear.

Ping! Ting! Clink! Ging!

The nun chucks, saitachis, dagger and katana hit the ground right after its wielders did. All six men were lying scattered on the ground with bruises and cuts appearing like magic on their faces and shit. With them out of commission, their ally was left to fight Anton head up.

The last men standing circled one another counter clockwise. They were locked into an intense stare down, studying one another carefully and trying to figure out their next moves. The man with the guillotine held his lengthy chain at one end while he winded the deadly end of his weapon up with the other. Abruptly, Anton stopped where he was and narrowed his eyelids at him. The nigga with the guillotine did the same, but kept on winding his weapon up. The young hitta cracked a smile and blew him a kiss. His opponent's face twisted with anger and he unleashed a battle cry, launching the guillotine in his enemy's direction. The guillotine came zooming towards Anton's face. He jumped up in the air and kicked that shit, sending it speeding right back at its welder. The man's face contorted in excruciation as he was cracked dead in the face by his own weapon. The assault left a red bruise behind and sent him sailing back. He hit the surface and flipped over on his stomach, sliding across the ground. Grimacing, he attempted to get up several times, but he had been too weakened by the fight to do so. He tried to push up off of the ground and went slamming back down into it. The defeated man took his last breath and blew debris up in the air.

Present

"All that for me, huh? I'm impressed." Fear said after Eureka finished telling him the story.

"You murdered our father, Alvin. My brother has a hatred for you that burns like a thousand suns. He's not going to stop until you're dead." She made eye contact with the killa through the rearview mirror.

"What about you? How do you feel about me?" he held her gaze in the rearview. She looked at him with an expression that he read easily. "I see. Does he know about this?"

"No." Eureka said in a hushed tone and turned the rearview mirror away. Right after, tears were sliding down her cheeks and she was sniffling. Although Fear couldn't see her, he could hear her. He bowed his head, feeling remorseful for what he had done. If he could take back what he did, he would in a heartbeat. Life doesn't work like that though. There isn't a rewind button. You have to live with the decisions that you make.

Hearing his cell phone ringing inside of his pocket, Fear whipped it out and looked at its screen. The letter N was on the display. Silently, he cursed and held the cellular to his chest, thinking of what he was going to say before he answered it. Staring ahead at nothing, he took a deep breath.

"Fuck it." He said to himself before answering the call. "'Sup?"

"I trust everything is on schedule." Nero assumed.

"I'm afraid not, I sent your boy ahead. I got caught up in some shit and had to bail."

"What? What're you talking about?"

"If you can say what then you can hear. Yo' ass ain't that old."

"Watch yourself now. Tell me what happened."

"I'll give you the short version…"Fear went on to give him a summary of all that happened up until Raymar made his getaway. Afterwards, he listened to Nero curse up a storm and throw something into the wall that shattered. "If you trained this man than you can bring him down. Go after him. I'll make it an even million dollars if you bring Raymar back to me."

Fear shook his head and replied, "No can do, pops."

"Why in the fuck not?" he asked irately.

"My son's been kidnapped and I have to see about getting him back in one piece. As of now, his wellbeing is of the utmost of importance to me."

"A son? I didn't know you had a son." He stated with surprise.

"Yeah? Well, I didn't either up 'til today."

"Listen, can you tell me in what exact direction was Ray headed?"

"Yeah," Fear gave him the route in which Raymar was headed. Listening and holding the telephone to his ear, Nero's hand moved swiftly as he jotted the information down on a sheet of paper. Once he was done, he dropped the ink pen down on his desk top and picked the sheet of paper up, looking over it while holding the phone to his ear. "You got it?"

"Yes, I have it."

"Okay. Listen, I'm sorry I couldn't deliver this time around. No hard…" Fear looked at his cellular having heard the line click like the Brazilian crime boss had hung up on him. That's exactly what he did. "Hello? Hello?" he looked at the device's screen and saw call ended on it. Shrugging, he said, "Fuck him and his snitching ass son."

***

"Motherfucking insubordinate," An angry Nero talked shit to no one in particular as he dialed someone up. "Good help is so goddamn hard to find these days. If I still had my youth and not this bum leg, I'd be out there busting my ass to get things done myself." He placed the telephone to his ear, cradling it with his shoulder. Listening to the ringing in his ear, he tapped his cane impatiently.

Twenty minutes after the call was made

Vroooom!

A black leather clad man in a helmet on a black Kawasaki Ninja flew up the street, riding alongside that white line in the road.

Vroooom!

A second man dressed the exact same way as the first one came speeding up behind his partner.

Vroooom!

A third man came speeding up on his motorcycle. After him there came another and then another and then another. All six of these men were dressed exactly the same and riding the same style motorcycles. Their bikes squealed loudly as they whipped around vehicles in traffic and dipped in and out of lanes, following behind homeboy that was at the head of their pack. Loose trash and debris came rushing into them and wafting at their backs, floating just above the ground.

All of the men's necks were on swivels as they looked around for the cat that they were looking for. Their leader slowed his motorcycle down coming across a Honda that lay toppled on the side of the road. It was surrounded by a tow truck and a couple of police cars that had their emergency lights flashing, their images shown on the black tinted visor of his motorcycle helmet. The leader of the motorcyclists looked to his right and saw someone far away in the distance on a motorcycle. Someone in a jail uniform was riding on the back of the bike. From the color of the jumpsuit the leader knew that the person had to be Raymar and the nigga with him had to be the cat that had taken him prisoner. Making his own assumptions, the leader pointed across the way which got all of his comrades to look. Seeing that he had their attention, he motioned for them to follow him, taking off on his motorcycle in that direction.

Vroooom! Vroooom! Vroooom! Vroooom! Vroooom! Vroooom!

The motorcycles flew down the street one after another, leaving debris and loose trash up in the air.

***

Anton pulled up in the driveway that the pickup truck was parked in. He dismounted his motorcycle and whipped out a pair of handcuffs, cuffing Raymar to the handlebars.

"Stay put, I'll be right back," Anton talked to him like he was a dog, wagging his finger in his face. Right after, he hauled off and cracked that mothafucka in the face, breaking his nose. Blood squirted and oozed down his lips and chin. The blow nearly knocked him off of the motorcycle but he held fast.

Raymar grabbed his bleeding nose and frowned. When he spoke his voice sounded muffled, due to his palm over the lower half of his face. "Fuck was that for?"

"For making me chase yo' bitch ass. Now, shut the fuck up." Anton smacked the shit out of the back of his head and hung his helmet on the opposite handle bar. After that he walked off, heading for the house that he had in mind. He came up the steps and stopped at the front door. Placing his fist to his mouth, he cleared his throat and knocked on the black iron door. He tapped his foot and looked over his shoulder at the street. Besides a couple of kids out riding their bicycles, there wasn't anybody outside. Looking from the kids, Anton came back around to Raymar. He was touching his bloody nose and looking at his palm, which had a smear of plasma on it.

"Cock sucka broke my fucking nose," the Brazilian fugitive frowned, talking to himself.

Hearing the black iron door coming unlocked, Anton turned back around just in time to see the door being pulled open. Before his eyes stood a Mexican man with a shaved head, he was wearing a blue jumpsuit that had oil smudges on it. The Vato appeared to be a mechanic. His sleeves were rolled up to show his tattooed hands which were still slightly stained with oil despite him washing them thoroughly. The Mexican man, whose name was Rico, adjusted his glasses and munched on the food that had formed a ball on the left side of his jaw.

"'Sup, foo?" Rico threw his head back and continued to munch on his food.

"Watts up, homie? Sorry to bother you, but you think I can use yo' jack to call Triple A? My bike broke down on me." Anton presented him with his most jovial smile.

Rico stared at Anton as he munched his food. It appeared as if he was studying the baby face killa to see whether he was full of shit or not. For all he knew his young ass could be from a hood that his gang beefed with coming to earn a stripe. He wasn't trying to be a notch under a mothafucka'z belt, fuck that.

Not able to come up with a decision, Rico figured it was better to be safe than sorry.

"Nah, homeboy, there's a payphone eight blocks up at the gas station," he moved to shut the door, but then Anton's hand shot up, freezing him stiff. The Mexican man's eyes lit up and he adjusted his glasses to make sure that was a stack of money that he was holding up. Indeed it was.

Anton looked around before going on to speak. "Look, I can tell you ain't for the Okey Doke. I know that money talks and bullshit walks a thousand miles. So, here it is," he shook the stack of money. "Here's the truth. I really do need to use yo' phone to call Triple A 'cause my bike broke down. See, I'ma bounty hunter and I'm running in this cat sitting on my bike over there," he kept his eyes on Rico and threw his head to the left. The Mexican mechanic looked to his driveway and saw Raymar's bloody nose ass sitting on Anton's motorcycle. The Brazilian fugitive cracked a smile of embarrassment and waved at him. "I'm really not tryna walk this cat eight blocks, man. Hell, anything can happen in that distance, you feel me?" Rico nodded. "Okay. Look, this is two racks. I'll give you a stack now to use yo' jack and the other stack once Triple A arrives and takes a look at my ride. Cool?"

"Cool," Rico opened the door and held out his hand. Anton took one thousand dollars from the two that he had and hesitantly laid the money into the Mexican mechanic's palm. He watched as homeboy licked his thumb and counted the dead presidents. Satisfied, he motioned for the baby face killa to come inside of the house. Stepping aside, he allowed him in over the threshold and locked the door behind him.

***

Raymar looked into the side view mirror of the motorcycle, seeing a half of a dozen of leather clad men on Kawasaki Ninjas flying up the block. He then looked over his shoulder; the men were closer than they appeared in the mirror and they were all armed. Acknowledging this, the Brazilian fugitive's eyelids stretched wide open and he gasped. He went crazy yanking his wrist back and forth on the handlebar of the motorcycle. Pain shot through his wrist and a red ring formed on it. He clenched his jaws and continued his yanking. Seeing that he wasn't getting anywhere with this strategy, he threw his good leg over the bike and kept yanking. He stopped for a second and looked to the leather clad men. The leader of the pack was pointing to the house that Anton had gone inside of. This alarmed him greatly, his heart quickened inside of his chest. He spit on his wrist and used the saliva to lubricate it. Holding the handlebar, he pulled his wrist into him trying to slide his hand out of the handcuff. His form slightly shook and he bit down on his bottom lip, pulling with all of his might. Before he knew it, his hand came loose from the cuff and he was falling back on the ground, bringing the motorcycle along with him. He withered in pain for a minute and then he went on to push the bike off of his injured leg. Hopping upon his good leg, he hobbled to the backyard of the house that Anton had gone inside of. Coming to the back widow of the house, he lifted up the window and climbed inside.

***

Rico showed Anton where the telephone was and stepped into the kitchen to grab the chicken and rice he was eating earlier. When he picked up the paper plate of food, his Taurus .9mm was revealed lying on the table top. He stood facing Anton's back as he pretended to dial up Triple A, letting his hand creep towards one of the .45 automatic handguns that was stashed on him. He was just about to whip around when all hell broke loose.

"It's a hiiiit!" Someone called out.

Anton looked up to see Raymar hobbling towards him as fast as he could.

Choot! Choot!

Bullets whizzed through the picturesque window sending glass flying everywhere. Rico's eyes widened and his mouth stretched wide open. Two red dots at the center of his jumpsuit quickly expanded. He staggered backwards and plopped to the floor like a fish out of water. Anton knew that the heat was on and the last thing he needed was Raymar's dumb ass getting killed before he collected that check that was on his head, so he tackled him to the floor. The snitch winced having had the wind knocked out of him from the young hitta when he fell on top of him. After rolling off of him, Anton whipped out both of his .45s with the silencers on them, telling Raymar to hide while he took care of the opposition. Raymar nodded and crawled on the floor down the hall, dragging his raggedy ass leg along with him. He pulled himself inside of the bathroom and shut the door behind him. He then crawled inside of the bathtub and pulled the shower curtain shut. Quickly, he said a prayer and crossed himself in the sign of the crucifix.

A loud crash against the window glass caused it to cobweb and drew Anton's attention. By the time he turned around the glass imploded and he saw one of the motorcyclists breaking the glass with the butt of a chrome .9mm with a silencer on its barrel. This was homeboy that had capped off Rico. The fool was about to blast on Anton but the young hitta got the drop on him. He squeezed off rapidly and gave it to him all in his mothafucking chest. When the nigga'z blood hit the broken glass it made it look like rubies in the sunlight. He fell to his death outside, dropping the shotgun not too far away from his hand.

Ba-Boom!

The front door came flying open and hanging off of its hinges, two more motorcyclists came through, guns blazing. Anton did a cartwheel over the couch and landed on his side with a thud. Hearing the motorcyclist coming for him, he sat one of his .45s on the couch's cushion and pushed it towards them, ducking down. As the couch absorbed the shots that were meant for him, he extended his .45 automatic handgun and squeezed off furiously, taking both of them niggaz the fuck out. When they hit the floor, he shot to his feet and walked around to the opposite side of the couch. He dropped his spent .45 at his feet. It was there that he found one of the gunmen still alive and attempting to point his gun up at him. Casually, Anton reached over the couch and picked up his .45 from off the cushion. He pointed that bitch at the lone survivor and emptied the magazine out on him with extreme prejudice, blood spotting his boots. Suddenly, the two windows inside of the living room imploded and two more motorcyclists came climbing through them. Seeing that his life was in danger, Anton ran out into the garage with them following not too far behind him.

Inside of the garage, Anton's head whipped around from left to right trying to find something to defend his self with. On the wall at the far left of him he found two machetes, going across one another to form an X. He ran over to the wall and drew the blades, one by one. He did fancy maneuvers with the weapons and they made whistling sounds through the air.

His movements told his enemies how skilled he was with the blades. Still maneuvering the machetes, Anton made his way in the man's direction. He was swinging his blades around so fast that they looked like flashes of gleaming silver. Seeing that he was in immediate danger, the man reached for his waistline and came back up with a gun, pointing it at him. He had just pulled the trigger with one of the machetes cut through his muscle and bone, causing his severed hand to fall to the floor, firing his gun. The man hollered out in agony, that thing at the back of his throat shaking. Blood squirted from out of his stump. He went to punch Anton and he cut off his remaining fist before he could connect. Right after, Anton swung around like a ballerina, doing a 360 degree turn, bringing his machete around with him. It ripped through the muscle and bone of his enemy's neck, sending his severed head high into the air. The face of the head held the expression of its owner still screaming. The body fell first but the severed head came last, smacking down on its side on the floor.

Just then, another one of the motorcyclist appeared in the doorway, pointing a mini AK-47. The assault rifle vibrated in his hand as he cut loose, empty shell casings flying high into the air, looking like blurs. The deadly weapon spat flames and the shell casings fell to the surface, sounding like loose change. Anton dove to the floor beside a station wagon, line of fire following right behind him. Bullet holes appeared on the side of the wagon like magic and its windows shattered into pieces, its tires bursting on flat. Lying on the floor, Anton saw the shooter reloading. Seeing his chance to act, he flipped over the hood of the wagon and threw one of his machetes. It spun around super fast and embedded its self into its target's chest. The motorcyclist's arm went up and his finger involuntarily pulled the trigger of the mini AK. The assault rifle spat fire and caused debris to fall from the ceiling. The man fell to the floor dead, staring off into space.

The baby face killa was so occupied with his victim that he didn't even notice Raymar hobble past the doorway as quietly and as fast as he could, en route to the front door.

Anton ran over and snatched his machete from out of his victim's chest, wiping his bloody blade off on him. Afterwards, he crept up the steps and made his way inside of the house. As soon as he turned in he got a chest full of pellets from a big ass shotgun. The impact of the lethal weapon caused him to stagger backwards, nearly falling. Having recovered, he charged forward and chopped off his threat's hand. As soon as his hand hit the surface, he got slashed across the neck and a river of blood spilled down his chest. His eyes were as wide as silver dollars and his mouth was wide open. When the man went to grab for the young hitta, he side stepped him and chopped off his remaining arm. Once it hit the surface, he kicked it out of the way and brought his machetes across one another. This action split his threat's stomach open and his intestines spilled out, splattering hard onto the floor. The motorcyclist dropped to his knees where he lingered for a time and fell flat on his face.

Bloom! Bloom!

Still holding both machetes, Anton stumbled forward from the shotgun blasts to his back. He whipped around and took a swipe at the shooter but he wasn't anywhere near him. In return, he got a full blast to the chest that sent him flying backwards. He fell on top of the glass coffee table and it exploded into pieces. He lay there still, holding the machetes in his hands. Cautiously, the shooter moved in on him, shotgun aimed at his chest. He got about one foot from Anton when his eyelids suddenly snapped open. With a grunt, Anton stabbed the blade into his foot and pinned him where he was. He threw his head back screaming loud enough to awake the dead. Anton came back up and chopped off the arm of the motorcyclist that was holding the shotgun. He then stabbed him in the chest with the machete and yanked the other one from out of his foot. Next, he stabbed him in the lower abdomen and lifted him above his head with the machetes. The motorcyclist hollered aloud and he threw his ass across the room, shattering the living room window on his way out of it.

Anton stood in the living room floor holding the machetes in his hands. He looked like a mad man with the spots of blood covering his face and upper body. His head was on a swivel as he breathed hard, chest rising and falling. He was looking around for any more threats that may be trying to stop his pulse. Unbeknownst to him, a lone motorcyclist crept up behind him and pointed his Desert Eagle at his back. He was about to pull the trigger when gunshots rang out inside of the living room.

Bloc! Bloc!

The sudden gunshots startled Anton and he whipped around, finding the motorcyclist that was about to pop him lying dead on the floor. He looked in the direction that the shots had came from and found Raymar behind the trigger. He was mad dogging his victim, both hands wrapped around the .9mm Taurus that Rico had left on the table top. His eyes darted from his kill and landed on Anton, turning his gun on him. Seeing that homeboy had the drop on him, the baby face killa didn't show any fear. Still holding the machetes, he slowly advanced in Raymar's direction, blood dripping from off his blades.

"Stop right there or I'll shoot chu!" Raymar threatened, clenching his jaws, veins bulging at his temples.

Anton completely ignored this mothafucka and kept on walking in his direction. Just as old boy was about to pull the trigger, Anton knocked the Taurus out of his hand with his machete. The gun fired as it went flying across the room and sliding across the kitchen floor, wedging its self beneath the refrigerator. Right after, Anton kicked him hard as shit in the chest, impact sending him slamming back up against the wall, creating breakage in it the image of a cobweb. Raymar slid down to the floor wincing and in a daze. Throwing down one of the machetes, Anton rushed over to him and snatched him up to his feet. He pinned the mothafucka against the wall and lifted his machete. Raymar squeezed his eyelids shut and snapped his head to the right, just as the machete was drove above his shoulder. This startled his cowardly ass and he trembled uncontrollably. Next, the baby face killa grabbed the Brazilian fugitive by the collar of his jumpsuit and looked him dead in his eyes.

Anton's pupils looked like two burning suns as he gritted angrily. "If it wasn't for the fact that you had such a large bag on yo' mothafucking head, I'd cut chu from yo' asshole up to yo' appetite. You fucking pussy," he hawked up a glob of saliva and spit in his face. Next, he gave him a punch to the gut that knocked the wind out of him and dropped him on his ass to the floor. "Stay here, bitch, I'll be right back."

Anton left the living room and came back with a change of clothes and a woman's wig, which belonged to Rico's girlfriend. He held the machete on Raymar as he got dressed in the clothing and wig. Afterwards, the young hitta grabbed the keys to the Toyota. He loaded his motorcycle into the back of the pickup and made Raymar get behind the wheel at gunpoint. As soon as homeboy cranked up the Toyota and drove off, police car sirens filled the air en route to the crime scene.

Chapter Four

"Ugh!" Tristan grimaced. He fell to the floor seeing double. Getting off his back, he scaled the floor, moving towards the door of the garage. All he could hear was the flames of the fire as they licked at the air and the sound of his heart beating in his ears. Its beating was in the beginning of thumping slower and slower, but that didn't stop him though. Nah, Tristan was determined to get to that mothafucka that had snatched his son up. Pushing open the garage door, all that could be seen was the light of the kitchen which was shining at his back, leaving him a silhouette. Tristan crawled down the cement steps and left a smear of blood behind him. He struggled to pull himself upon his feet by the Ford Explorer that was parked inside, but once he was standing, he felt a sense of accomplishment. Holding onto the back of the SUV, Tristan took a good look at his surroundings. Once he spotted the tool box in the corner of the room on top of the table, he peered closer and saw the silver duct-tape peeking out at him. His eyes zoomed in on it and it seemed to be calling his name. He knew exactly what to do with this. Now, he just had to get his hands on it. Tristan took the time to remove his shirt. While doing so, he noticed the blood that had slicken his hands and the wound the arrow created. Looking down, he saw droplets of his own blood pelting the cement floor and his shoes.

"Shit." Tristan cursed under his breath. He felt light headed and saw double again, his legs buckling underneath him. He squeezed his eyelids shut and locked his jaws. A vein bulged at his temple as he did this. Homie was trying to will himself to do what he had to do. "Okay." He looked back up at the tool box and took several quick breaths. With that done, he began his journey towards his destination. At the halfway mark of reaching the tool box, his legs buckled again and he almost fell. Having recovered before he could meet the surface, he pushed on and moved forward on wobbly legs. When he felt like he was going to fall again, he swiftly grabbed a hold of the tool box and placed half of his weight against the table. Taking the duct-tape out of the tool box, he used it to wrap his torso until he felt like he wouldn't bleed through it. Unbeknownst to him, his bloody hands had stained the duct-tape red with his fingerprints. Tristan threw the roll of duct-tape aside and fished his keys out of his slack's pocket. Having unlocked the doors of his truck, he staggered forward and until he met the driver side door. Quickly, he unlocked the door and slammed it once he'd jumped inside behind the wheel. He pressed the button on the remote control that was clipped to the sun-visor and fired up the Explorer. He revved up the humungous vehicle and floored it, burning rubber from off the garage floor. He left black tire prints around in his wake. Tristan gripped the steering wheel with both hands as he flew across the lawn of the grounds of the estate.

Tristan blinked his eyelids repeatedly, finding his self growing faint from his loss of blood. His head wobbled and he peered closer to the windshield. Before he knew it the wall of the estate near the gates had grown closer than he remembered. He turned the steering wheel to his left before he fainted and the rear end of the Explorer slammed up against the wall. His head slammed up against the steering wheel just as the airbag exploded, giving his forehead a cushioning for a soft landing.

***

Eureka pressed the button on the gate opener that was clipped to the sun-visor. The gates of the mansion opened inward and she drove inside across the threshold. Looking to her side view mirror, her eyeballs nearly leaped out of their sockets when they saw the Ford Explorer mashed up against the wall and Tristan's face planted into the airbag.

"What the fuck?" A panicked Eureka brought the Impala to a stop and hopped out, leaving the door wide open. Fear sat up in the backseat and threw open the door, running to where Eureka was headed. He came to her side as she was opening the door of the crashed SUV. She pushed Tristan back against the seat and examined him, making sure that he was alive. Looking down, she saw the hole in his side and the blood that had soaked his shirt. A line creased her forehead and she looked to the mansion, remembering that her son was inside. "Fear, look after him, I've gotta go check on Kingston." She ran towards the mansion as fast as she could. "Oh, please, God, please, let my baby be alright." Head tilted back and fists clenched, she sprinted across the lawn, chest thumping up and down. "Haa! Haa! Haa! Haa! Haa! Haa!" she huffed and puffed out of breath, closing the distance between her and the estate. Reaching the bottom step, she leaped upon the porch and darted inside of the mansion. She saw the blood on the wall where her husband was impaled and then the arrow on the carpet. Seeing the legs of the maid laid out in another doorway, she darted into the room that she was in and came upon her bullet hole riddled body. She bowed her head and crossed herself in the sign of the crucifix. Afterwards, she wandered throughout the mansion calling out her son's name, checking each and every room. When she couldn't find him, she came down the staircase and walked over to the living room couch. Plopping down, she placed her hands to her face and broke down sobbing. Her shoulders rocked back and forth, as she shed tears.

"Reka! Rekaa! Reekaaaa!" Fear called out her name repeatedly.

Eureka's head snapped up and she ran to the doorway. She found Fear holding Tristan's arm over his shoulders and holding him at the waist with his other hand. The somewhat dead weight of the man was pulling the already weakened killa down, but he was struggling to keep them both upon their feet. Seeing Fear struggle with her husband, Eureka came running out of the mansion and down the steps. She moved like the wind blew, running across the enormous lawn of the estate. Fear and Tristan collapsed on the lawn by the time Eureka reached them. The killa got back upon his feet, helping his former student pull her man back upon his feet. They held an arm each over their shoulders and they trekked back to the mansion, heading inside of the kitchen. While Eureka held Tristan up, Fear walked over to the table and smacked all of the items off of it. He then helped her walk her husband over to it, his bending legs dragging across the floor. Together, they hoisted him up and lay him on the table top. Fear tore open his shirt and sent button flying everywhere. He took a good look at his wound, seeing that he was bleeding badly.

"We're gonna have to plug this before he bleeds to death." He announced to Eureka. His brows furrowed once he noticed that she had a worried look on her face. "What? What's wrong?"

Slowly, she brought her head up, showing her crying eyes. She wiped the tears that trickled from her eyes with her curled finger and said, "He's…he's gone. Jesus, I can't find my baby." She rushed over to him and hugged him tightly, trembling as she shed tears. He brought his muscular arms around and embraced her against his chiseled chest, wincing from the beating he'd taken earlier that day from Anton.

"He…he took 'em…" Tristan said. His face was shiny and he looked pale, both hands lying over his wound. Eureka's eyebrows rose and she broke her embrace, pulling away from the killa who she'd thrown herself into.

"Who? Who took 'em, baby?" Eureka ran over to the table, caressing his forehead lovingly.

"Some…some…some British mothafucka dressed in a costume," he told her. She looked from him to Fear and then back again. "He killed the maid, shot me with an arrow and kidnapped King. The...The son of a bi...bitch said he was looking for...for you."

"Me?" Eureka's forehead wrinkled. She and Anton had made many enemies over the years so the list of who wanted her head was a lengthy one. So she couldn't narrow it down to who the cock sucka was that had hit her family.

"N...No." Tristan shook his head, wincing. He then lifted his bloody hand and pointed his finger at Fear, "You."

Fear and Eureka's foreheads crinkled, they exchanged glances and then looked back to Tristan.

"Me?" Fear pointed a thumb at his chest. A look of confusion crossed his face.

"Yeah."

"Fuck he want with me?" he frowned.

"I don't know. But since King is your biological son, I assume that he's gonna use him to get to you."

"Oh my, God," Eureka gasped, bringing her hands to the lower half of her face. "No. Nooo." She said with her eyes wide and lips trembling. A million scenarios raced through her about what the man that had kidnapped Kingston could be doing to her son at that moment. Eureka imagined her baby boy crying his eyes out for her and his father to save him. She saw him scared, hurt, all alone and wanting to be home. The thought of him being in that condition racked her with such great emotions that it was overwhelming to her. Little momma felt like she was about to snap and lose it. There wasn't any doubt in her mind that she could go on without her son. He meant too much to her.

Seeing Eureka crying, Fear wrapped his arms around her and pulled her close. He whispered in her ear that everything was going to be okay. Tristan shot him a disapproving look and he gave him an expression that let him know that it wasn't even like that. He wanted to contest, but figured now wasn't the time to take it there with him, considering the circumstances and his condition. With his wound, he wasn't in any condition to fight. He was sure he'd be an easy win for his opponent.

"What this nigga look like, family? You get a name or seen a tattoo?" Fear questioned.

"He was muscular and dressed up like a mercenary…and…and he had an accent. That's what really stood out to me about him, his accent. I can't say for sure where it's from, but if I had to I'd say it would be British, England." till holding Eureka in his arms, Fear looked off to the side, forehead wrinkled and eyes wide. From the expression on his face, you could tell that he was thinking about something.

A hitta from England? I don't know any head busters from England. Fuck could this nigga be?

Eureka snatched away from Fear, realizing that she was allowing him to hold her in his arms. Her husband knew of her history with him, so she knew that he'd be in his feelings having seen such a moment. When she looked to Tristan he was still wincing and holding his hand to the area of his body that had been wounded. It appeared as if he wasn't even paying attention, but she knew that he must have seen something. They were standing right in front of him.

Fuck, a bitch gone really hear it now. I can't say that I blame him though. 'Cause if the shoe was on the other foot I'd be on his ass like stink on shit. Trist isn't gone let this ride, I'll be prepared to deal with this later.

Eureka turned back around to Fear, wiping her face with the lower half of his shirt. "Do you know of any hittas from England that may have taken King?"

The killa shook his head no and her shoulders slumped. "No, I'm afraid not."

"Ex…excuse me…but…but does anyone care that I'm bleeding to death here?" Tristan said. He was sweating and had a pale complexion, looking like he was about ready to pass out due to blood loss.

"Holy shit, I'm sorry, babe. I'm so caught up with what happened to our son."

"Eureka, you gotta first aid kit here?" Fear asked.

"Yeah. It's inside of the bathroom under the sink."

"Bring it. I'ma patch up this wound of his as best as I can until my guy makes it up here. You got any scratch here?" he asked her of money that she may have stashed inside of the mansion.

"Yeah."

"Good. My guy doesn't come cheap but he's worth every penny." He told her. "Lemmie borrow your cell right quick." She tossed it to him and he hit up the doctor that had patched Anton up that night he was wounded when they took out Niles Bemmy. Fear gave the doctor the address and thanked him before disconnecting the call, sitting the cellular on the counter. At this time, Eureka had already gone off to retrieve the first aid kit.

Fear leaned his back up against the kitchen counter and looked him in the face.

"Do you still love her?" Tristan inquired of his feelings for Eureka.

"Look, bruh, what we had is long gone." Fear told him straight up.

"That's not what I asked you."

Placing his hands on his hips, Fear looked up to the ceiling and took a deep breath. He then looked down at Tristan and said, "Yeah...I still love her, but there's notta chance for us. She knows that. She has a family and I'm still caught up in the life."

"Yeah, well, you just remember who wife she is," Tristan lifted the hand of the finger that wore his platinum wedding band.

"I'll try to." Fear headed out of the kitchen to go take a piss.

"What was that?" The Dominican scowled.

"I said, fuck off." Fear said from over his shoulder, continuing out of the kitchen.

Chapter Five

When the doctor arrived, Fear assisted him in bringing in the equipment that he'd need for Tristan blood transfusion. They set the medical stuff up inside of the guest room and retrieved the bags of blood that they'd need for the procedure. Afterwards, the doctor prepped the Dominican for the blood transfusion. Tristan's blood type was AB so that made him a universal recipient, meaning he could receive blood from all donors. This made it easier on the doctor because he didn't have to pay his plug a little extra to get an exact type of blood.

Once the transfusion was done, the good doctor left Tristan some pain killas and advised him not to drink alcohol with them. He told Eureka to make sure that he got plenty of rest, received his payment for his services, and was walked to the door by Fear. After seeing the doctor off, Fear made his way to the bathroom to shower. Eureka had given him a change of clothes. They belonged to Tristan so she was sure that they'd be a little baggy on him but they were better than having nothing at all to wear. Hell, it wasn't like he could fit that nigga Anton's clothes, they were of two completely different builds.

Tristan lay in bed looking exhausted, flipping through the cable channels with the remote control. He was in black silk pajamas with his initials on the breast pocket. His top was opened to his muscular hairy chest and his torso was gauzed and bandaged. A small crimson dot was on his peach colored bandages. This was the area of his body that had been pierced by Julian's arrow.

"Can I get chu anything, handsome?" Eureka asked from where she was leant up against the doorway, arms folded across her breasts.

"Nah, I'm good." Tristan said, steadily flipping through the channels. The nigga didn't even bother to look her way.

"You sure? Something to eat or drink? Anything? How about a hookah? I know where baby bro's stash iiiisss." She sung, a big smile stretching across her face.

"I'll pass. I'm not really in the mood to get high."

A frown crossed Eureka's face; she'd never known her husband to turn down a chance to get 'nice'.

Eureka pulled up a chair and sat beside her husband. Leaning closer to him, she outstretched her hand to caress his forehead but he turned away. That's when she knew that something was definitely up with him.

"What's the matter?" A crevasse deepened her forehead. She was genuinely concerned.

"What was up with that shit about with ol' boy in the kitchen?" his brows furrowed.

"What're you talking about?"

Tristan sat up as best as he could and looked to her. "You hugging up on this nigga. That's what the fuck I'm talking about." He spat heatedly.

Fuck! I knew this shit was coming. I just didn't expect it now.

"That wasn't about nothing, baby. I was hysterical about our son. I couldn't seek comfort from you in your condition, and he was right there. I'm sorry, Tristan. I didn't mean any disrespect." She reached for him and he snatched his hand away from her.

"Bullshit! I can't believe you played me in front of that nigga, Reka. You know how bad that makes me look? Huh? Anotha man seeing that he has my wife in her mothafucking feelings?"

"It ain't even like that, Tristan." She spoke with sorrowful eyes.

"Did you forget that you told me that chu still got feelings for this mothafucka? Now, you may have not meant to do what chu did, but subconsciously you couldn't help yo' self. Your inner feelings betrayed you and made me look like a weak ass nigga. And ain't shit weak about this Dominican," He slapped his hand up against his chest.

"You're right," she nodded. "I did tell you about my feelings for him. I love you but there's also a part of me that desires him."

Tristan was looking her dead in her eyes when she said this. Before he knew it he felt a hot stinging in his pupils and his eyes pool with tears. Although he blinked to fight them back, what his wife had just said stabbed him through the heart. Now, physical pain was something else, but emotional pain…emotional pain was a bitch. That was for damn sure.

Tristan squeezed his eyelids shut and swallowed the spit in his throat, pulling himself together before he spoke. He was in his feelings now, so he knew that if he spoke before he'd gathered his wits he'd fall apart in front of the love of his life and he couldn't have that under any circumstances.

"So…" he began, peeling his eyelids back open and swallowing the ball of hurt that had formed inside of his throat. "How do you think that makes me feel knowing that my wife…the woman that I gave my last name to in front of God Almighty," he looked up to the ceiling and outstretched his hands, his wedding band visible on the ring finger of his right hand. "Has feelings for anotha man that she hasn't seen in four goddamn years." He threw the remote control across the bedroom and it deflected off of the wall. When he turned to Eureka tears were sliding down his cheeks and hers. Sniffling, she wiped her tearing eyes with her curled finger.

"I can't say I know how you feel, but if…if I were you…to know that my significant otha loved someone else besides me…it…it would destroy me."

"Right…and that's exactly what it did," he wiped his eyes with the hand that wore his wedding band. He then took a deep breath and blinked his red webbed eyes. Looking to her, he continued what he had to say, "You're gonna have to make a choice though."

"What're you saying?" she asked curiously.

"You're gonna choose between me and Mighty Mouse there," he pointed a finger at the door. "You're gonna have to choose, right here and right now. I need this love triangle to come to an end. If you dump me, then I wanna move on and allow my broken heart to mend its self."

"Tristan, now is not the…"

"Nah, fuck that! I wanna know and I wanna know now," he jabbed his finger downward, eyebrows sloped and nose wrinkled. His nostrils were flaring and he was quite angry.

Eureka shut her eyelids briefly and swallowed the lump of anxiety in her throat. "Okay…alright…I'll choose. I want to be with…"

"What's going on here?" Fear asked from the doorway. He was in a plaid shirt, Levi's that hung slightly off of his ass and All Star Chuck Taylors. An indention was in his forehead as he looked back and forth between Eureka and her husband.

"You," Tristan mad dogged him, his pupils burning with fire and his lips twisted. "I shoulda smoked yo' ass back in that van when I had the drop on you, but I'ma man of principles so I allowed you to keep yo' life."

"I guess that's a regret that you're always gonna have to live with, 'cause that will be your first and last time ever having me before your gun again. 'Cause let me tell you, family, had it been me behind that trigger, Eureka would be making your funeral arrangements."

"Bitch ass nigga," Tristan spat, his top lip twitching with animosity.

"If you see a bitch then hit a bitch, you pretty mothafucka!" Fear unfolded his arms and entered the bedroom.

"You ain't said nothing but a word, homeboy," Tristan threw the blanket off of him and attempted to get out of bed but he was still weak. He knees buckled but he kept himself up, making his way towards Fear so that he could get in that ass. Seeing him trying to approach, Fear came walking towards him. The killa had his eyebrows arched and his jaws squared, fists balled at his sides.

Eureka looked between both men that she loved frantically; she didn't know what to say or do.

Tristan stormed towards Fear. As soon as he reached him he swung on him twice and did a Round House Kick. The killa dodged the attack swiftly. When he came back up he kicked his ass dead in the mothafucking chest. The impact from the kick sent his ass hurling backwards, flipping over the bed and slamming his head back against the wall.

"Fear, stop! Stop!" Eureka hollered aloud, jumping in front of Fear, trying to push him back.

"Move, Eureka, move! This is what this mothafucka wanted so I'ma give it to his ass," Fear growled and shoved Eureka aside, she fell up against the wall and bumped her head. She winced and rubbed the back of her head.

With Eureka out of the way, Fear unbuttoned the sleeves of his shirt and rolled up his sleeves. He started in Tristan's direction. He couldn't see him behind the bed but he knew that he was there. The killa hadn't gotten halfway across the room when Tristan came charging at him. Before Fear could mount a defense he was getting tackled and picked up from off of the floor. Tristan ran as hard and as fast as he could, slamming him into the wall and then throwing him to the floor. The assault took a lot out of the Dominican, especially with his wound having weakened him. Still, he had to put an end to the brawl fast or he ran a risk of losing. And he couldn't have that.

Tristan lifted up from off Fear and rained blow after blow on his face, busting his shit up. Blood speckled Tristan's pajamas and stained his knuckles. Looking back up at his opponent ignited a fight in Fear's pupils and he punched that mothafucka dead in his wound. This drew a howl of pain from homeboy and he grabbed his side. While he was occupied with his stinging side, Fear jabbed him in his eyes with his fingers. He hollered aloud, that thing at the back of his throat shaking. He fell over onto the floor bawling in pain. Seeing his enemy at a disadvantage, the killa scrambled upon his feet and pulled Tristan up to him by the collar of his pajama shirt. He then drew his arm back and formed his fingers into a set off claws. His eyes darkened with hatred and he clenched his jaws so hard that veins bulged at his temples.

Eureka shook off her daze and looked to Fear, seeing him about to finish off her husband with his kill-move.

"Feeeaaaar, noooooooo!" she called out to him, knowing what he had in mind.

Fear looked past Tristan's wincing face and looked down into his left peck. It was like he had X-Ray vision because through his eyes he could actually see his beating heart. He knew exactly where to strike in order to rip his fucking heart out of his ribcage. With a grunt, Fear moved to tear Tristan's heart from out of his chest and pull it loose from its valves. His fingers had just sunk into his enemy's chest when Eureka grabbed him by his wrist, staring him in his eyes, pleadingly.

"Please," she said, on the verge of tears again.

Fear looked from her crying eyes to Tristan's chest, red bruising had formed around the fingers that he had sunk there. Taking a deep breath, the killa took his hand from off of the Dominican's peck and let him fall to the floor. Staring down at him, he used his tongue to feel around inside of his mouth and then he spat out blood to the side.

"It's outta love and respect for Eureka that I'ma allow you to keep yo' life, homie. It's because of that and the fact that I don't take any pride in killing a man that's in a bad way. I'll tell you what though, if you still got in mind that you want a piece of me once that wound of yours heals up, we can settle this shit head up."

"You…you got it," A wincing Tristan looked up at him with tearing eyes. They'd grown watery from Fear poking them.

"Alright. Now, let's put this bullshit aside and see what we can do about getting baby boy home in one piece," he outstretched his hand to him. Tristan looked from the killa's hand to Eureka. She gave him a nod and he looked back up at the killa, searching his eyes for any signs of deceit. Once he saw that there wasn't any, he grasped his hand firmly and allowed him to pull him back upon his feet.

"Now, you said that the security cameras were scrambled by some kind of the device that he had, right?" Fear started the conversation with Tristan like he hadn't just tried to kill him a second ago.

"Yeah, that's the only way that I can explain how the cameras and the rest of the electronic devices here went out and wouldn't come back on. The nigga had to have had something that disrupted everything." Tristan winced as he rubbed on his bruised peck.

"Did the security cameras have something that they were recording to? Say like a video or DVD?"

"Yeah, everything is filmed onto a disc, we change them every day." Eureka interjected into their conversation.

"Great. Eureka, you gotta laptop? If so, can you upload your security system software to it?"

"Unh huh," she nodded.

"Smooth. I want you to get the software and the disc."

"What do you plan on doing with the disc?"

"I have a hunch on who's behind all of this. If the nigga that snatched lil' man is who I think it is…we may have a lead."

With that having been said, Eureka darted out of the bedroom to retrieve the items that Fear requested. She was back in no time with the laptop and the software was already loading on it. Once the software had been loaded, Fear uploaded the DVD footage of the day that Julian had stormed the mansion and snatched up young Kingston. Tristan understood how the software worked better than anyone besides Anton so they allowed him to do what Fear had in mind.

Fear stood off to the side with his eyes focused on the laptop which was Tristan's lap. Eureka lay in bed beside him watching the screen of the laptop also.

"You said he entered through the front gates, right? Well, show me all of the camera angles of him at the gates." Fear told him. "Ah, there we go. Now, try this camera's angle right here." He pointed to the square that he desired. Once Tristan brought the square up to fill up the laptop's screen. "Beautiful. Now, zoom in on the face of this fucking fucker."

"Okay." Tristan replied, his finger tips punching the lettered keys. He punched one more button and the still image of Julian King grew bigger. The image was a little grainy but everyone got a good look at the nigga idling at the front gates of the estate.

"There we go," Fear said and looked to Eureka's husband. "Is that the asshole with the British accent that snatched up junior?"

"Yeah," Tristan nodded, eyes focused on the screen. "That's the mothafucka." He locked his jaws and the skeletal bone structure shown in them. A thick vein throbbed at his temple also. Just seeing the UK assassin on the screen caused his wound to ache.

Fear stood up and began pacing the bedroom back and forth, massaging his chin. Eureka and Tristan focused on him, watching him attentively and wondering what the fuck was on his mind. Suddenly, the killa stopped and rubbed his hand down his head of waves. Taking a deep breath, he turned around and faced the married couple.

"This guy that we're discussing that busted down the gates and took Kingston, I think I know who he is now."

Eureka and Julian exchanged glances and then looked back to Fear.

"Well, who the fuck is he?" Eureka asked, sliding off of the bed and approaching him.

"He's a British, England hit-man by the name of Julian King. One of the best in the business from what I understand." He informed them.

"Who hired this clown? That's what I wanna know." Tristan's face balled up.

"Annabella Bemmy." Fear answered.

"Annabella Bemmy? Isn't that…" Eureka was cut short by the killa nodding.

"Yeah, that's her, Niles Bemmy's daughter. I can't say that I'm surprised. I got word from the streets that The West Coast Connection hired him to take me out, but homeboy got caught up in some shit and didn't make it out here in time."

"How do you know for sure that it was Niles' daughter that hired that British faggot?" Tristan inquired.

"I don't leave any loose ends untied. Although I'd taken up residence in Rio, I had eyes and ears out here watching homegirl. She's taken over her father's empire, and has risen in status and power. The lil' bitch has a hard-on for me. I got word that there was a hitta out here looking for me but I wasn't worried about it 'cause I wasn't in the states. I had it in mind to take daddy's lil' girl out once I wrapped up the gig that brought me back out here. I was gonna send my employer's son back home on his father's private jet and go looking for her ass." Fear walked over to the wall and leaned his head back up against it, staring up at the ceiling. "My guess is that this Julian King character took your son 'cause he knew that I was his biological father. Since the nigga couldn't find me, he snatched my bloodline to draw me out and kill me."

At that precise moment, Eureka's cellular rang. The entire bedroom fell silent. She reached inside of her pocket and pulled out her cell phone, seeing that it was a blocked number.

Normally she didn't answer blocked calls, but something told her that she'd better answer this particular call.

"Hello?" Eureka answered, eyes moving around. At this time, Fear and Tristan was focused on her, wondering what was being said over the phone.

"Why hello there, dis is must be da startlingly beautiful Eureka I presume."

"Who is this?" her forehead creased.

"I'll give ya a hint, I have a liddle somethin' in my possession dat is very near and dear ta ya heart. How's dat?" a smile stretched across Julian's face, as he continued to pace the floor in front of a sleeping Kingston. The boy was asleep in a fetal position on the tattered twin mattress.

"King?" her eyes lit up.

Tristan and Fear exchanged glances. The Dominican frowned and shuffled over to Eureka, snatching the cell phone from her.

"Look here, homeboy, you done fucked up snatching that one there. That boy of mine comes from a lineage of killaz. Now, you're one person, there's strength in numbers. Not only do you have his motha to deal with. You got his uncle, his fatha and his biological fatha to contend with. That's right, you British faggot, you gotta whooooole family of killaz that'll be on yo' ass if we don't get King back. So, I suggest…"

"I suggest you shut ya fuckin' trap right dis minute before I drench ya child wit gasoline and set him on fiyah." Again, a smile stretched across Julian's face, and he waited for Tristan to say something else. He didn't utter a word. The line was so silent that the UK assassin thought that the Dominican had hung up. "I thought so. Now, ya mention dat his biological fatha is there, I'd like ta speak wit him please."

A defeated express was plastered on Tristan's face as he took the cellular from his ear and held it out to Fear. The killa pointed his thumb at his chest like *He wants to talk to me?* The Dominican nodded and he took the cell phone.

"Put it on speaker so that we can hear him." Eureka said in a hushed tone to Fear.

Fear nodded and cleared his throat, holding his fist to his mouth. Afterwards, he pressed the speaker button on the cell phone and held it away from his face, looking down at the screen as he talked.

"Yeah," He spoke, eyes looking from Eureka to her husband and then settling back on the cell phone.

"Ah, finally, da man I have been killin' and kidnappin' ta see. How are ya, Al?"

"Fear is fine. I'm okay, but I'd be doing a lot better if I had my son."

"I'll tell ya wut…you want ya son back and I want chu. Ya come ta me alone and I'll let da liddle fellow go in one piece. Ya show up wit anyone else and I'll gut da liddle fucka like a fish. How's dat?"

Fear looked to Eureka and saw the pleading in her eyes and her tear drenched face. She had her hands together like she was begging. She mouthed to him to please go along with the deal. Little momma didn't have to plead with him though. Nah, he was going to go along with whatever Julian wanted to get Kingston back. Although he hadn't laid eyes on him, he was still of his flesh and blood and he didn't want to see any harm come to him.

"You still there?" Julian asked.

"Yeah, I'm still here, family. You gotta deal. Where do you want to make this exchange?"

"Hold up," Tristan snatched the cellular from out of Fear's hand and pressed it to his ear. "Here's the deal. I'll give you myself in exchange for King."

"No deal."

"What chu mean, no deal?" Tristan's forehead crinkled.

"Wut are ya deaf? No fuckin' deal, bruvh. Now, put da otha chap back on da phone." The British executioner got angry. "Annoyin' fucka he is." He said to himself as Tristan passed the cellular back to Fear.

"Yeah," Fear came back on the line.

"Do me a fava, Fear, don't eva put dat fellow on da phone again. I don't care ta speak ta him…eva."

"No problem." Fear glanced over at a scowling Tristan. He was holding a worried Eureka in his arms, running his hand up and down her back soothingly. "Yeah, I gotta pen." The killa glanced at Eureka and snapped his fingers, motioning for her to retrieve him an ink pen. Eureka broke her husband's embrace and darted over to the dresser, searching it for an ink pen. Her eyes spotted a gray & black Sharpie marker. She grabbed it and tossed it over to Fear. He snatched it out of the air and pulled off its cap with his teeth. At this time he was already listening to the address that he was being given, luckily for him he had remembered most of it. Hurriedly, the killa jotted down the address inside of his palm and looked it over.

"Ya got it, chap?" Julian inquired.

"Yeah, I got it." He answered, putting the cap back on the Sharpie marker.

"See ya then." The UK assassin disconnected the call.

Fear handed the cell phone back to Eureka. She took it and looked at the address that he had written on his hand with the Sharpie. She knew exactly where the meeting location was and so did Fear and Tristan.

The address belonged to a neighborhood that they remembered hearing about in the news years ago. The particular community was under quarantine from a flesh eating virus that had broken out. It was said that three hundred people had died from the infestation. Some from the sickness and others from the lethal bullets of the CDC whom were trying to keep them contained within the neighborhood so that they wouldn't get out and spread the deadly virus. The Center for Disease Control was able to get the situation under control, but no one dared to live within the community for fear of catching the disease. The way they saw it, it was better safe than sorry.

"I gotta call baby boy and let 'em know Watts up." Eureka pulled out her cellular and hit up her brother.

"Watts up, sis?"Anton picked up on the third ring.

"King's been kidnapped." She informed him. Her eyes welled up with tears when she broke the news to her brother.

"What? By who? You tell me who snatched my lil' nigga up and I'ma hunt that mothafucka down, on daddy's grave."

"A British assassin by the name of Julian King, he shot Tristan with an arrow, slaughtered the maid and took your nephew. We know where he's at but we need your help."

"Whaaaat? Is brother in law straight?" he asked with concern.

"Yeah, he's fine. Fear had his doctor friend check him out."

"Good. Now, what part do I play in this sitch (situation)? "

"Like I said, we know where he's at. Fear's gonna meet up with him to exchange himself for King, but we all should be there lurking in the shadows to make sure we get 'em back once we get King."

"Okay. I'm with the shit, slide me the address." Anton told her. She obliged him. "Alright, I got it."

"The drop goes down in an hour, thanks, baby boy."

"Stop with that thanks bullshit, sis. We family, and family takes care of one another, you feel me?"

"Respect."

"Tadowl."

"Where are you?" Fear came on the line.

"I'm at where I'm at and I'll be where I'll be. Fuck you won't, nigga?" Anton's attitude changed instantly hearing his old sensei's voice.

"You still sitting on my bag?"

"You talking about Raymar? Yep, I'm finna collect on his bitch ass too."

"That money was mine." Fear gritted.

"That's right… was. Now, his ol' ratting ass belongs to the kid. Don't worry though, 'cause after I'm done collecting this check that's on his head, I'm on yo' ass, my boy. We gone definitely settle up what we started a ways up the road, you feel me, my nigga?"

"You're that anxious to die, huh?"

"Hahahahaha, don't be so sure, old man. I've learned a lot more than what you've taught me, please believe me. In fact, I think I may have one up on you."

"Hahahahaha," Fear gave a throaty laugh and then he suddenly shut up, voice growing serious.

"Daniel Son could never fuck with Mr. Miyagi, it'll do you some good to remember that, lil' nigga."

"I hear you talking, dawg, but chu gotta show me better than you can tell me, catch my drift?"

"Oh, we gone definitely lock ass."

"I'm looking forward to it. Now, put my sister on the phone."

"Hold on."

"Fuck you very much."

"Hello?" Eureka came on the line.

"Yo, after I take care of this lil' business, I'm on that thang we spoke about. I don't won't chu to worry about nothing. Bro bro gotchu faded."

"Okay."

"I love you, Reka."

"I love you too, baby boy."

He disconnected the call.

Eureka stashed her cellular inside of her pocket and turned around to Fear.

"Listen, I appreciate you all tryna gather the cavalry, but I gotta go solo on this one."

"You can't go alone. Julian's definitely gonna kill you once you get there." Eureka stated.

"I know. But if he finds out that I didn't come by myself then he's gonna put the love on King, neither of us wants that I'm sure of it. " He looked into the married couples eyes and their looks assured him of this.

"Look, man, we aren't the best of fucking friends. In fact, once all of this is over, I plan on beating the living shit outta you and I can't do that if yo' lil' ass is dead. You going up there to holla at homeboy alone is like a cow walking himself out to be slaughtered. It's suicide." Tristan stated. "Let us make this move witchu."

"You don't have a choice, there's no sense in any of you arguing with me 'cause I'm going alone. I don't give a rat's ass if you like it or not, you feel me?" Fear's eyes bled his seriousness as he swayed his finger from Eureka to her husband. Taking a deep breath, he shut his eyelids and ran his hands down his fade. "Look, besides, I gotta 'nother mission I need y'all to roll out on." He reached inside of the small pocket of his Levis.

Eureka and Tristan exchanged glances.

"What mission are you talking about?" Eureka asked curiously.

With that said, Fear tossed a USB chip over to his former student. She snatched it out of the air, pulling it down in her fist and bringing it closer. Opening her palm, she saw exactly what it was and a line creased her forehead. She looked up at his old comrade with a confused expression etched across her face.

"The blueprint to Annabella's building are on that chip there," Fear pointed to the USB chip in her palm.

"Where'd you get this?" Eureka frowned.

"I have my resources." He responded.

Fear had put in a call to a plug of his that was a man of many trades. He could get you any and everything. He could also have someone hit for the right price. The gentleman and his network had a very exclusive clientele and they dealt with very few. Fortunately, the killa was one of those chosen few. He used his contact to get him the blueprints of Annabella's building.

Flashback/ Woods

The night was silent, besides the crackling of the burning camp fire. The golden orange flames of the fire illuminated Fear as he practice martial arts moves, looking like he was fighting opponents that only he could see. Having worked up a sweat, he stopped and wiped his sweaty forehead with his forearm. His chest rose and fell as he breathed heavily. He sat down on a log and placed his palms together, reciting a prayer with his eyelids shut. Suddenly, he threw a punch to his left and struck something solid. The impact from the blow sent what he had hit tumbling backwards. When the killa's head snapped around to where he'd thrown the punch, he found a short Japanese man skidding to a stop, dust from the ground masking the air. He was dressed in tattered jeans and a wool poncho. He'd lost his large straw hat in his tumbling. The Japanese man scrambled upon his feet, grabbing his staff and hat. He dusted the hat off and placed it back on his head. Next, he switched hands with the staff and took off running at Fear. The killa got into a fighting stance, fists raised and legs spread apart.

The Japanese man flipped high over his opponent's head as he threw a punch. Coming over his head, the little man struck him in the back of the head, back, side and hip bone. When he landed on his feet he struck him in the back of the knee, dropping him down to one knee. Following up, he jumped up and kicked him hard as shit in the temple. The force behind the kick sent Fear falling down on his side. He breathed heavily, causing dust to go up in the air. Hearing a battle cry and the shifting of air that came with swift movement, Fear's eyes darted to their corners. He saw the little man go up in the air, holding his staff high above his head and his knees at his chest. He was about to come down hard on his opponent's chest, on some Bruce Lee shit.

Fear moved out of the way at the last minute. When the Japanese cat came down on his bending knees, dust flew up into the air. His head snapped to the direction that Fear rolled off in and found him moving to sweep kick him. Swiftly, the Japanese cat flipped over his leg and landed on one bending knee. Right after, Fear was on his little ass, throwing a series of punches and kicks that his opponent deflected and dodged with some trouble. He ducked the last kick that came at him. When his head came back up, his chest was met with a clenched fist. The blow caused the little mothafucka to buckle and he went hurling backwards. He slammed up against the car the killa was using to transport Raymar in and cracked the back window into a cobweb. The Japanese man fell to the floor, losing his straw hat and his staff. Moaning, the shorter man slowly began to rise to his feet. Fear was on him quick though, kicking him in his side and making him howl in pain. Once he fell on his back, he was stomped in the stomach so hard that he felt the wind being forced out of his lungs.

Fear snatched up his opponent's staff and held it at his throat, staring down at his wincing face. The Japanese man had a crown of silver hair and a goatee. He was old and had wrinkles all over his face that showed his age.

"Fuck are you?" Fear asked, eyebrows sloped and jaws squared.

"Uuuhh," The little man moaned in pain.

"You better start talking fast before I crush yo' fucking throat." The killa threatened.

"I'm...I'm Chochi. I came to bring you this," he reached beneath his wool poncho and pulled out something that looked like a clear plastic pill bottle. Inside of it was a USB chip. The hostility drained from Fear's face. He took the staff from Chochi's neck and relieved him of the small bottle. He looked

at the USB chip inside of the bottle and then back at the man he'd taken off of his feet. He then pulled him upon his feet and handed him his staff. Afterwards, he picked up his straw hat and dusted it off, sitting it back on the little man's crown of silver hair.

"Where the fuck is Lester?" Confusion crossed Fear's face.

"He's busy with something else, so he sent me."

"My sincerest apologies, I assumed you were here to take out my employer's son," Fear nodded to Raymar. He was sound asleep on the ground, the glow of the crackling fire shining on his face. The son of a bitch had slept through the entire fight between Fear and Chochi.

"No. Believe me, if I had been sent here on a mission to kill anyone...he'd be dead and you'd met with your Maker before you realized what happened to him." Chochi assured him, brushing the dirt from off of his clothing.

"I believe you. You're pretty nice with yours," Fear referred to his fighting skills and then looked at the bottle again. "You sure all of the info I'm looking for is here?"

"Yes," he nodded.

Having been given reassurance, Fear slid the bottle inside of his pocket and pulled out a bankroll of money, which was secured by a rubber band. He tossed it over to the Japanese man. He caught it and reached beneath his poncho, sliding on a pair of reading glasses. After he popped the rubber band on the money, he looked the blue face bills over carefully to make sure that they were authentic. Satisfied with his inspection, he put the glasses away and stashed the money inside of his pocket. He then bowed to Fear and he bowed back. When the killa brought his head back up he frowned, the little man had vanished into the air. Forehead creased, Fear looked up, down and all around for him. When he realized that he was gone, he shrugged and made his place on the ground to lie down. Shutting his eyelids, he drifted off to sleep. He needed all of his rest because he had the task of transporting Raymar back to the plane that would take him back to Brazil the next day.

Present

"You sure this is her building?" Eureka asked Fear.

"Yeah, Annabella bought out this entire building that her father leased a space in. OG was using the place as a front to have his business meetings. He didn't trust any place else 'cause he didn't know whether they were bugged or under surveillance. Anyway, lil' momma bought the entire building. She rents out a few spaces but that's just to keep the law from snooping around. She actually uses the tenement to distribute kilos from. Her supplier transports the drugs there in UPS vans and she ships off the quantities to her clientele. Homegirl doesn't trust anyone, which is why she's there every time a delivery is made. Once the coke is delivered, she takes her leave."

"What do you want us to do?"

"What I trained you to do." Fear looked her dead in her eyes.

"Kill her?" Tristan spoke what the killa had in mind.

Fear looked to him and nodded. He then looked to Eureka, "Take her out and make sure that shipment goes up in smoke. Can you handle that?" She nodded. He looked to Tristan and he nodded as well. "Good. While y'all busting lil' momma's shit up, I'm gonna see to it that King makes it home to his ma and pa." he looked at the married couple, smiling. "Guess I better change, never know what may go down."

"Indeed." Eureka gave him a nod.

Fear returned the gesture and moved for the door. He turned back around when Tristan grabbed him by his arm, lifting an eyebrow.

Tristan leaned closer to him and said, "I'd like to thank you for what chu doing here. You know, offering yourself up in exchange for our son? Although y'all share the same bloodline, you don't have a bond. You could have been like fuck that lil' nigga but you didn't. Thank you." The killa gave him a nod and moved to leave, but the Dominican held fast, causing him to turn back around to him. "That tussle back there between you and me…it's far from over, homie. Just as soon as I recover and we get my son back…you and me are gonna dance. Oh yeah, we're gonna do The Tangle, know what I mean?"

Fear snatched his arm away from him and mad dogged him, wrinkles forming across the beginning of his nose. "You can count on it, Hector." He put the emphasis on his name.

Tristan stuck his head out of the doorway and looked down the corridor, seeing Fear's back as he strolled down the hallway, "It's Tristan…you hear me, nigga? Triiissstan!" Nostrils flaring and chest jumping, the Dominican turned back around and found Eureka staring at him. She was looking at him like she couldn't believe that he was behaving how he was right then. Shaking her head, she made her way towards him.

"Excuse me, I gotta go get ready," Eureka said brushing his shoulder as she walked past him.

Chapter Six

Having reached his destination, Julian murdered the engine of his Cadillac and hopped out. He slammed the door of his vehicle and walked around it, boots crunching on the graveled ground. He unlocked the trunk of the old car and lifted it, casting light on Kingston. The little dude's eyes narrowed against the illumination of the day, as he struggled with his restraints. When he looked up and saw his captor mad dogging him, fire dancing in his pupils. The hit-man stood there staring at the boy, appearing only as a silhouette to him. He tilted his head to the right as he observed him, then suddenly, he unsheathed a Bowie knife. When the sunlight kissed the blade a gleam swept up the length of it and it twinkled at its tip. Although his heart rate sped up, Kingston's eyes didn't display any fear. He had been trained by his uncle to never show such an emotion when in danger by the hands of an enemy. Julian brought the knife forward and sliced the duct-tape from the boy's ankles. He then pulled the gray tape off of him and flapped his hand until it came loose, falling to the ground. He went on to slice off of the duct-tape from his wrist as well. Next, he pulled a length of chain from his belt that was attached to a pair of handcuffs, which he used to restrain the youth. Grabbing him by the front of his shirt, he lifted him out of the trunk and sat him down on the surface. The assassin's shadow cast on him as he slammed the trunk shut. When he turned around he found the boy staring up at a filthy white mansion that was tangled in vines. Its front lawn was covered in tall dead grass that looked like hay. The roof of the place had large holes in it that would allow rain to fall through and slick the floor inside. There wasn't another home surrounding the mansion for miles.

Standing where he was, Kingston took in the scenery. The sun beamed brightly from the sky, beating down on him. He hadn't been out of the trunk five minutes before he'd broken a sweat under the intense heat. Already the little nigga was planning his escape. His train of thought was broken when he felt a tug on the chain that pulled him forth. He damn near tripped and fell the pull was so strong, but recovered before he could hurt himself. Kingston was lead along by Julian. They made their way through the tall golden grass, with the assassin chopping it down with a machete. When he reached an old rusty reddish brown gate that was at the end of a driveway, he forced it open with one powerful kick. The gate squeaked and squealed as it swung open, scratching up the ground as it flew inward. Julian led Kingston into the backyard where there were two broken down cars and a motorcycle. One of the car's hoods was open and its engine was missing. The backyard was just as unkempt as the front. It had tall dead grass too, but that didn't slow the hit-man down. He chopped a path through it with his machete, leaving the golden grass in his wake. Julian looked up at the back door breathing heavily, chest inflating and deflating. Sheathing his blade, he approached the back-door and kicked that bitch open, sending a spray of splinters across the kitchen.

The loud noise sent a rat scurrying across the filthy floor. Cobwebs were everywhere and so were spiders. The golden rays of the sun shined at the assassin's back, highlighting the dusty furniture and appliances that were left behind. Looking into the living room, Julian saw the large sun spots casting down on the floor from the large holes in the ceiling. Everything around it was slightly lit or hidden within the shadows. Julian took the time to spit off to the side before lumbering forth, his leather boots squashing a cock roach he hadn't notice. When he crossed the threshold into the living room the dusty hardwood floor squeaked, sounding like it was about ready to collapse under the weight of the hit-man.

Julian located an old dusty mattress in the corner of the room, not far from a radiator. Grabbing a hold of the chain that bound Kingston to him, he trekked across the floor in the direction of what he had his sights set on. He directed the boy to the mattress and chained him up to the radiator. Afterwards, he ruffled his head and made his way to the living room closet. Here, he pulled out some flood lights and a speaker system. With this system, niggaz would be able to hear his voice loud and clear, like it was coming from a helicopter or some shit. It took some time, but he set up everything just outside of the mansion. He worked up quite a sweat once he was done, wiping his shiny forehead with the back of his hand. At this time, he made his way around to the back of the mansion. En route, his cellular rang and he answered it through his Blu-Tooth.

"Ah, Ms. Bemmy, it's a pleasure as always," Julian smiled evilly, showcasing his beige teeth he'd gotten from years of smoking.

***

The sun beamed brightly on Annabella as she stood in the backyard of her enormous mansion. She was in a wife beater and spandex pants. Her hair was pulled back in a pony tail and her hands were covered in black gloves. Her body glistened from the intense workout. Her heart pounded and her chest inflated and deflated with each breath that she took.

Each swing of the katana sent beads of sweat flying from off of her body. Her sword whistled as it was swung through the air, back and forth. She moved like a fucking ballerina with the lethal weapon. The warm rays of the sun made her look like she was glowing, that golden orange illumination outlining her form.

What in the hell is up with Julian? I haven't heard back from him yet. I surely do hope that he is as good as my associates' say he is. I can't go on living another day knowing that my father's killa is still out there. That son of a bitch has got to pay and he owes me his life. That's for damn sure.

Annabella swung her sword one last time, holding the post that she made when she came around. She stared ahead at nothing, breathing heavily. The arm holding the katana was extended out and her freehand dangled at her side. Having finished practicing for the day, she dropped her hand at her side and headed for the back entrance of her home. Along the way she pulled out her cell phone and called up Julian King, pressing the button that activated her Blu-Tooth. The phone rang three times before Julian finally answered it. As she talked to him she pulled open the glass siding door that lead into her house and into the kitchen. Shutting the door back, she went on to make herself a healthy milk shake. She blended carrots, tomatoes, celery, asparagus, etc. Once she was done, the blender was full of a thick green substance and the outside of it ran wet, looking like human sweat.

Annabella grabbed a glass from out of the cupboard and filled it with the green substance. Taking the time to clear her throat, she took the glass to the head, drinking it like she was thirsty. When she was done, she licked the residue off of her lips and rinsed out the glass, sitting it back inside of the cupboard.

"You got some news that's going to make me smile, Mr. King?" Annabella inquired.

"I surely do." She heard the saliva moving around in his mouth as he smiled devilishly. "I got da lion's cub in my possession and I'm sure it's gonna draw 'em out. And when it does, well, let's just say dat you'll be gettin' a phone call dat you've been lookin forward to fa a while now."

"Now, that's what I like to hear. I'll be looking forward to your call. Talk to you then, Mr. King." She disconnected the call.

***

"You hungry?" Julian asked Kingston. The little nigga mad dogged him and twisted his lips, looking like he wanted to bite his fucking head off. Although he didn't respond, his stomach growled which said it all. He was starving. "Ah, I figured as much. Here ya go, bruvh," he dropped the McDonalds bag on the filthy mattress. Cautiously, Kingston crawled over to the bag, keeping his eyes on the UK assassin the entire time. Swiftly, he snatched the McDonalds bag and crawled over as far as he could from him. He took out the cheese burger and the fries sniffing them to make sure he didn't smell anything funny. He was hungry as hell but he wouldn't allow his hunger to lead to his death, which was why he was giving everything a thorough inspection. Quickly, Kingston removed the wrapper from off of the cheese burger and bit into it. He devoured it and crammed the fries into his mouth. Keeping his eyes on the man that had taken him hostage, he munched on the food. Abruptly, he started coughing and choking on the meal, eyes growing teary. Seeing this, Julian offered him some of the soft drink that he had in his hand, but the boy declined it. Figuring that the youth didn't want it because he feared that it may be poisoned, he took a sip from the straw and offered it to him again. Kingston snatched the cup from his extended hand and pulled off the lid, taking it to the head thirstily. The dark brown soda spilled down his chin and stained his shirt as he guzzled it, throat moving up and down his neck. He brought the cup from his mouth and wiped his lips with the back of his fist, tossing the empty cup aside.

"Here," Julian sat down two buckets and a roll of toilet paper. He pointed to the respective buckets, telling Kingston what each one was for. "Da fust bucket there is fa ya ta take a deuce and da otha there is fa ya drizzle. Da toilet paypa there is two ply. It's da good stuff too, Charmin. One thousand sheets a round or somethin' or otha. Not like dat cheap crap dat tears before ya finish wiping ya ass." He stood there for a moment, staring at the youth like he was waiting for something, tapping his foot impatiently. Kingston just sat there looking at him with his wet and crumb riddled chin, wondering what the hell he was just standing there for. "Well…" Kingston gave him a look that said What? "Aren't cha gonna thank me fa bringin' ya somethin' to nibble on and ya toilet paypa?"

"Thank you." Kingston spat like he didn't really want to.

"Ya welcome," he reached for his head but the youth moved back, thinking he was going to try to hurt him. The British executioner's hand stopped where it was, and then slowly moved forward, finally ruffling Kingston's head. With that done, Julian walked off whistling Dixie. He sat down on an old ass milk crate and whipped out a rag to polish his Desert Eagle. While he was handling this task, his cell phone rang. He stopped and pressed the button that activated the Blutooth headset. There was only one person that had the number to his cell phone so he already knew who it was.

"Hello?" Julian answered the call.

"Mr. King, I hope you have some good news to report to me, sir." Annabella told him.

"I sure do, Ms. Bemmy."

"Well, wow me."

"Let's just say dat I have a lil' somethin' dat's gonna draw our friend out from where ever he may be," he looked over his shoulder at Kingston. He found him playing with a mouse. Afterwards, he focused his attention back on the conversation at hand.

"Now, that just put a big smile on my face."

"Glad to hear it. I'll get in touch with you once the job is done."

"Very well, I'll be looking forward to your call. Talk to you later."

"Bye, bye." Julian disconnected the call. He went back to polishing his Desert Eagle but stopped momentarily. His forehead deepened with lines and he looked over his shoulder.

Kingston's ass was gone. "Fuck me!" he sprung to his booted feet and shoved the Desert Eagle into its holster. Next, he drew his machete and stormed through the living room, heading for the kitchen. It was there that he saw the backdoor cracked open, a silhouette moving past it in a hurry. "Liddle fucka," he took off running through the kitchen and kicked the backdoor open. Looking ahead, he saw Kingston making hurried steps through the tall dead grass near the pool. The little nigga jumped onto the fence and threw up his leg, attempting to crawl over it. Seeing this, the UK assassin jumped down into the grass and went after him. He chopped down the dead grass that was in his way as he moved forward. Making it to the fence, he hopped over it with one hand and jumped down. He landed into the backyard of a house that looked just as shitty as the mansion that he'd just left. He saw Kingston disappear through the backdoor of the estate. Having taken note of this, he took off running after him. Making it up the steps, he tried to turn the door knob to enter but it was locked. Acknowledging this, he chopped at the fragile door with his machete. As he narrowed his eyelids, splinters flew into his face as he swung his sharp weapon repeatedly. Chest heaving up and down, he punched a hole where he was hacking at and reached inside, unlocking the door. Pulling his hand out, he kicked that bitch wide open. He was a silhouette standing in the doorway, sunlight shining at his back. His head whipped from left to right, looking for his hostage. When he didn't see him in sight, he slowly made his way through the kitchen, combing through everything with a fine comb. Having not come up with Kingston, he searched through the living room. He opened the closet door that was beneath the staircase and peered inside. The space was clear, save for a cobweb hanging before him, a spider crawling across it. As soon as he shut the door and turned around, a wooden chair came slamming against the side of his head. Broken legs and other parts of the chair went flying everywhere and Julian dropped to the floor. Dazed, he looked up and saw two blurred images of Kingston before him. Quickly, the youth picked up the machete that his abductor dropped when he struck him with the chair. The little nigga went to drive the machete through the UK assassin's chest, but he smacked the blade out of his hand and back handed him. The blow spun the little mothafucka around and he hit the floor, landing on his hands and knees. Shaking off his daze, Julian scrambled to his feet and advanced in Kingston's direction.

Kingston ran towards Julian, jumped on the end of the couch and leaped off of it. He flew into the British execution-er's face, swinging his small feet across his jaw. The heels of the youth's sneakers came fast as hell, sending blood and spit flying. The little nigga landed on his hands and shot right back up into the air, upper cutting Julian. The blow caused him to stumbling backwards. Kingston didn't stop there. Nah, he went charging and leaping forward, driving his sneaker into his chest. The force behind the impact sent the UK assassin slamming through the wall, legs hanging out of the hole that he was inside of.

Kingston stood where he was, fists up and legs holding the right stance, ready to finish the brawl that he'd started. His eyebrows were arched and his nose was scrunched up. He panted, chest rising and falling as his lungs filled with air. Moaning came from his opponent, who had slowly begun to stir inside of the wall. It wasn't long before he was pulling himself out of the large hole and shaking the plaster residue from off of his head. He stood a safe distance from Kingston holding his shoulder, which was dislocated. Knowing that he'd be no good in a fight in his condition, he walked over to the wall and slammed his shoulder into it. The impact knocked it back into place and made him holler out in excruciating pain, eyes tearing up. He placed his forehead against the wall and shutting his eyelids, taking a deep breath. His chest rose and fell rapidly as he breathed huskily. Swallowing the spit in his throat, he turned around to Kingston with an evil smirk on his lips.

"I've clearly under estimated you liddle one, it appears dat ya built fa da shit. Whoever trained you did very, very well. May I ask who it is dat I owe a salutation to?"

"My Uncle Anton, he's the best that there ever was…nobody can beat him." Kingston spoke of his kin confidently.

"I beg ta differ, at least not 'til I cease ta exist." Julian stood erect and lifted his hands, getting into a martial arts fighting stance. "Come on, ya liddle shit, show Uncle Julian wut ya got." He motioned him over with his hand. With that gesture given, Kingston took off running at him, screaming at the top of his lungs. He leaped into the air and did a spin kick, trying to take off the British executioner's head. Julian blocked the attack and the youth came back around with a solid punch to his jaw, which sent a ripple through his cheek and loosened his teeth. As soon as Kingston's feet graced the floor, he was up and at him with the quickness. His fists and kicks came in flurries, but the UK assassin dodged and reflected them with ease. He smiled as he was pleased with the boy's skills and courage. He expected him to be frail and afraid but he was sadly mistaken.

Kingston delivered a combo to Julian's midsection. When he dipped to the floor and tried to sweep kick him, the British executioner kicked him in the back of the head. The impact sent him flying into the wall, smacking his head up against it. The little nigga hit the floor, eyelids shut and a lump growing at the side of his head, he was knocked out cold. Breathing hard, forehead sweaty, Julian stalked over to Kingston and pulled him up the back of his shirt. The boy hung in midair slightly turning from side to side like he was hanging from a rope. Staring at him, Julian rubbed his jaw, feeling the aching it since Kingston had punched him in it.

"Impressive, liddle King. Ya only four years old now, but by da time ya fully grown, ya goin' ta be givin' ya opponents hell. Dat I promise." With that being said, he slung the little dude over his shoulder and located his machete, sheathing it on his side. Afterwards, he made his way back through the kitchen and out of the back door, heading back to the mansion.

That night

Eureka strolled inside of the guest room wearing a ninja's uniform and holding her mask in her hand, a black duffle bag slung over her shoulder. She was surprised to see that Tristan was dressed and lacing up his combat boots. Once he finished lacing his boots, he snatched up his duffle bag and slung the strap over his shoulder.

"Where are you going?" Eureka's brows furrowed.

"Wutchu mean, baby? I'm finna bust this move witchu." Tristan's forehead wrinkled.

"How in the hell are you gonna roll along on this ride in your condition?"

"Look, I'm coming along on this hit whether you want me to or not. I'll be damned if I stay behind and something ends up happening to my wife…mothafuckaz already snatched up my son, and I was denied the right to bang out on the British nigga that did it. My family is out in the streets, and should they die in them I wanna be right there beside them." He spoke from the heart.

Eureka took a deep breath and looked away, running her hand through her hair. She then looked back to the man that got down on one knee to propose to her. Nodding her head, she said, "Okay. Let's move." She stuffed her mask in the pouch of the duffle bag, leaving it hanging halfway out. She motioned for her husband to follow and he came up right behind her.

***

Anton sat in the front passenger seat, .32 pressed into Raymar's side. He casually looked around as his prisoner drove. The illumination from the light posts flickered on and off them as they drove underneath them, putting them in darkness and then light repeatedly.

Hearing his cell phone ringing and vibrating inside of his jacket, Anton reached into the recess of his jacket and pulled it out. A line creased his forehead seeing a telephone number with a weird number that he'd never seen before on the screen. Wondering who could possibly be calling him, he decided to answer it, keeping his gun in that nigga Raymar's side.

"Watts up?" he spoke into the cellular. Listening to what the caller was telling him, he glanced over at Raymar who was focused on driving. Seeing that his attention wasn't divided, Anton brought his attention back to the cell phone. "How much are we talking? Nah, that right there ain't gone cut it, fam. You gone have to come again, it sounds good but it's not good enough. Fuck I just say, nigga? I ain't got time for this shit. You either come up off 1.5 or no deal. Peace." He disconnected the call.

"Who was that?" Raymar looked back and forth between Anton and the windshield.

Anton's head snapped to him and he scowled, jabbing him in the side with his gun. A sharp pain caused Raymar to wince and wither but he kept control of the truck.

"Mind yo' fucking business, nigga, and stay the fuck up from outta mine," he took the banger from Raymar's side and pressed it to his temple. "Do we understand one another, Raymar?" he spat his name like it left a bad taste in his mouth.

"Yeah," the Brazilian fugitive nodded, wincing and rubbing his side. "We understand one another."

"Good. Now, shut the fuck up and keep driving."

Raymar straightened himself out and kept driving like he was told. The illumination from the light posts continued to flicker on and off them.

***

Raymar drove into the underground parking lot complex and killed the engine of the old truck. He passed Anton the keys and opened the driver's door, sliding out of the vehicle. The young hitta came out behind him and slammed the door shut. He then pressed his .32 into his back and led him to the elevator lobby. As soon as Anton pressed the UP button, the elevator made a ding sound and its doors parted. The men stepped inside and the doors shut. Before they knew it the elevator was stopping on their designated floor and the doors were opening again. Still held at gun point, Raymar was led down the long corridor, reflection shown on the marble floor. Glancing down, he saw Anton at the rear of him with his banger on him. This slowed him down, so the young hitta shoved him forward with his weapon and told him to keep moving. The Brazilian fugitive stumbled forward and nearly fell. Having regained his equilibrium, he looked over his shoulder and mad dogged the man that had taken him hostage.

"Gone and open yo' mouth so I can put a hot one through it, ya chatty mothafucka!" Anton dared him with a pair of threatening eyes. Unwilling to take the risk, Raymar turned back around and kept on walking. "Yeah, I thought so." At that moment his cellular rang and vibrated inside of his pocket. Pulling it out, he saw that it was the exact same asshole that had called him on his way up to see his employer. Sighing and rolling his eyes, Anton went on to answer the call. "Check this out, homeboy, if you can't do at least a mill and a half, you may as well hang up now." He listened to what the caller had to say and then a smile etched across his face. "See, now that's what I'm talking about. Once I get the confirmation that the first half has been deposited, I'll take the contract out. Smooth. Peace." He disconnected the call and stashed the cellular in his pocket. Looking up ahead, Anton saw two niggaz in expensive suits. These were the same two men that he had a confrontation with when he came to meet Frost. A grin appeared on Anton's face. He just knew that those two dickheads were going to give him a hard time again. And oddly enough, he was looking forward to it.

Anton stopped before the two niggaz in the suits outside of Frost's office doors. They scowled and folded their arms across their chests. These two remembered exactly who the fuck Anton was.

"Gentlemen, are we really gonna go through all of this again?" Anton looked between the two of them. They didn't say a word, so the young hitta went ahead and shot one of them in the foot. Fire ripped through the bodyguard's leather dress shoe and he grabbed it, howling in pain as he hopped around on one leg. Seeing the other bodyguard about to draw down on him at the corner of his eye, Anton swayed his gun from the cat he had shot and held it in his face. The bodyguard raised his hands up in the air and took a deep breath, bowing down to the youngster.

"Too slow on the draw there, my boy, now you get the same thang that cha man there got," Anton nodded to the bodyguard that he had shot in the foot and then he popped the un-wounded one in the foot too. The dick- head did the same thing that his homeboy did when he was shot in his foot.

"Argh!"

"Gaaah!"

The bodyguards squeezed their eyelids shut and threw their heads back, clutching their wounded foots. Anton smirked and tucked his gun out of sight. Afterwards, he opened the twin doors of Frost's office and walked inside, pulling the doors shut behind him. When he turned around he found that nigga Frost standing beside his desk with an AR-15 in his hands. Having heard his bodyguards howling in pain outside of his office doors, he grabbed the assault rifle and made sure its magazine was fully loaded. He'd just came from around the desk with his weapon when Anton and Raymar came waltzing in through the doors.

"Slow yo' roll, pops. It's just lil' old me." Anton told him, seeing the assault rifle in his employer's possession.

"What happened outside?" Frost wanted to know, hoisting his AR-15 at his shoulder.

"That outside?" he looked over his shoulder at the doors and then looked back to him. "That wasn't about nothing. I just had to show them fuck-boys you got working the door what kind of cloth a young nigga is cut from. They'll be okay, I promise."

"Good."

"Now, as you can see, I've got your package here," Anton kicked Raymar in his ass and he stumbled forward, nearly falling.

"Yes, I see," Frost smiled evilly, thinking of all the ways he could kill the piece of shit that raped and murdered his daughter.

"Now, about that check," Anton brought up his take for capturing Raymar to his attention, rubbing his hands together greedily.

"I've already sent you the other half."

"My man," The young hitta cracked an appeased smile.

Frost sat his AR-15 down on his desk top and advanced in Anton and Raymar's direction. When the Brazilian fugitive saw him coming, his heart thudded inside of his chest and he swallowed the lump of fear that had formed in his throat. He didn't have an inkling of an idea of what the old school gangsta had planned for him, but he was sure that he'd come to regret being born once he found out. That he was sure of.

Frost was in the shadows of his office as he moved forward, but the closer he drew to Raymar, the more of him that became visible. It started at his legs, his torso, his neck and then finally his face. His eyebrows were arched and his eyes glinted with evil, a devilish smile stretched across his face. He stepped to Raymar. The smaller man looked up at him like he was a giant, and he was compared to him. Before his ass could utter a word, Frost's hand was shooting out and grabbing him by the throat.

"Gaaaah," Raymar gagged and squinted his eyelids, feeling Frost's hand squeezing his neck. He became teary eyed and struggled to breathe, squirming in his powerful grasp.

"That's right you, lil' bitch, it's your turn to suffer," Frost's merciless eyes stared into the dying eyes of his victim as he clenched his jaws, veins throbbing at his temples. Anton stood where he was watching everything unfold. He could have gone about his business but he figured why miss the show. "Lemmie know when you see Jesus, nigga." Frost whispered into that nigga Raymar's ear, seeing the red webs etch in his eyeballs. Once the Brazilian fugitive began to turn blue in the face, Frost switched hands with him and whipped out his handkerchief. He draped the handkerchief over his victim's head and grabbed him by both sides of his head, beginning to squeeze. Raymar screamed weakly and put up what little fight that he could. He'd already been weakened from the choking so he didn't have much strength to thwart him off. "Unh huh, it was nice knowing you, ya fucking weasel!"

At that moment Anton's cellular rang and vibrated inside of his pocket. Keeping his eyes on the drama, he pulled out his cell phone and saw a text he'd gotten from the nigga he'd chopped it up with earlier. Seeing deal on the screen, he smiled mischievously and put his cell phone away. Right after, he outstretched his arms and triggered the mechanisms that drew both of his .32s into his palm from out of his sleeves. He aimed them at Frost, popping shots in his shoulders, bullet grazing his neck. His bald head ass released Raymar and fell back to the floor grimacing, gunshot wounds making him feel as if he was on fire.

"Aaaaah, sssssssss, damn," Frost squeezed his eyelids shut and gritted. Peeling his eyelids back open, but still withering in agony, he saw Raymar lying on the floor trying desperately to catch his breath. Not too far away he found Anton casually strolling in his direction, his twin pistols barrels wafting with smoke. "What the fuck is this? We had a deal, you lil' shit!" spit flew from off of his lips.

"Right, you paid me to bring you the snitch and I did exactly what I was paid for. That contract has been fulfilled." Anton told him. "Now, I must fulfill another one…" he pointed the twins at him.

"You fucking…"

"Rest in peace," Anton cut the gangsta's words and life span short.

Bop! Bop! Bop! Bop! Bop! Bop! Bop!

Frost did a little dance as the bullets flew into him, tearing up his suit and bloodying it. Studying his handiwork, Anton lowered his hands and triggered the mechanisms that drew his twin pistols back inside of his sleeves. He then turned around to Raymar and extended his hand. The Brazilian fugitive rubbed his throat and stared up at the young hitta's hand, teary eyed.

"Your old man saved your ass, coughed up that check at the last minute. He wants me to get chu on this jet tonight so you can make it back out to Brazil. Come on," he motioned for him to take his hand with the hand he was holding out to him. Taking a deep breath and throwing caution to the wind, Raymar grabbed his hand and allowed him to pull him back upon his feet. Just then, the double doors of the office came flying inwards and the cats that Anton shot in their feet stood there, attempting to lift their weapons. Before those mothafuckaz could pop off, Anton was tackling Raymar to the floor. As soon as he hit the floor, he rolled over continuously and activated his twin weapons. The pistols shot out into his palms and he aimed them, shooting flames. The niggaz in the suits did a short dance before falling to their deaths.

Anton lie upside down, eyes still on the niggaz that he laid down, twin pistols still trained on them. His chest rose and fell as he breathed. He got upon his feet and ejected the magazines, allowing them to hit the floor. Next, he loaded up fresh magazines into the .32s and pressed the buttons on his mechanisms to draw them back inside of his sleeves. Right after, he grabbed Raymar by the back of his collar, pulling him to his good leg.

Raymar looked around at all of the dead bodies lying on the floor. "Why…why did you off these guys? I thought you were with them?" his forehead wrinkled with confusion.

"Nah, see, you got it all fucked up. This right here was business," Anton's finger jabbed downward, referring to the hit he'd just put down. "Business doesn't have no loyalty. And I wasn't with these niggaz. I'm with who's ever got that bag. You feel me? Now, yo' daddy came outta pocket to make sure his lil' boy gets home," he ruffled Raymar's head and the criminal pulled away annoyed. "So, that's exactly what I'ma do, make sure yo' tattle tale ass gets home in one piece. Now, come on." He grabbed him by his arm and pulled him along violently, wearing a no nonsense expression across his face.

After making sure that Raymar made it on his father's private jet, Anton dropped by one of his outpost on the skirts of the city. He got suited, booted and armed himself with more guns. Right after, he found himself back on the road, en route to help rescue his nephew.

Chapter Seven

Tristan ripped up the street in the Ford Explorer, the illumination from the light posts aligning the curb playing on him and Eureka's faces. Looking over at her he could tell that she was worried about their son, and rightfully so. Things may not go as smoothly as Fear made it sound once he got to the designated location. And if they didn't it was a very good chance that neither he nor Kingston would make it back alive.

Tristan reached over and grasped his wife's hand. Lifting her hand, he kissed her tenderly on the knuckles and caressed her hand with his thumb. She looked at him and smiled. For the next couple of minutes the SUV was silent as the lovers were wrapped up in their thoughts. Finally, Tristan decided to break the ice.

"You still haven't given me your answer," Tristan looked from the windshield to his wife.

"What're you talking about?" Eureka's forehead crinkled.

"You neva told me who you chose outta me and homeboy back there," he threw his head over his shoulder.

"You right. I've gotta make a choice. I already know who I want so I don't even gotta think about it."

Tristan swallowed the lump of nervousness in his throat, his heart beat fast inside of his chest. He wanted to know who his wife had chosen to spend the rest of her life with. Although he felt that it should be him because he was her husband, he knew how she felt about the pint sized killa, even though he was the nigga that murdered her father.

Seeing Eureka peeling her lips open to say something, he stopped her by holding up his hand. "Hold up. I don't want chu to say anything, I'd rather read it." Tristan popped open the glove box and grabbed a slip of paper and an ink pen. He smacked the glove box back shut and passed the items to his wife. She took them. Holding the small slip of paper down on her thigh, she jotted down something and folded the paper up, stashing it inside of her ninja fit.

"You'll get your answer once we complete this mission." She told her husband.

"But what if…"

"Shhhhh," she hushed him, holding her finger to his lips. "Like I said, once this mission is complete, you'll know who I chose to be with soon enough."

With that having been said, Eureka focused her attention out of the front passenger side window. The scenery of the streets reflected on the glass window. Tristan looked back and forth between her and the windshield, heart thumping in his chest. Curiosity got the best of him and he was constantly wondering who Eureka had chosen to be with. If it wasn't him then it would crush his heart, but if it was him then he'd feel like the happiest man on earth…just like he did on the day Eureka said yes when he proposed.

Tristan took a deep breath and nodded, saying, "Alright. Okay."

***

Tristan coasted down the side street of the building that he and Eureka had planned to invade. The front passenger door popped open and Eureka hopped out, nearly falling. She hopped up on her bending knees and made her way across the street, hunched over. Removing her backpack, she took out the suction cups that she'd need to scale the side of the building. She slipped the backpack back on over her shoulders and took a good look at her surroundings before beginning her climb of the tenement.

Having let Eureka out in the middle of the street where he was sure that she wouldn't be seen under the guise of the night, Tristan looked over his shoulder through the back window. He'd turned around just in time to see Eureka crawling up the building like a spider. He smiled jovially and looked back around. At this time he saw a trail of UPS vans coming in his direction. He knew off top that these vehicles were carrying the kilos of cocaine that were to be delivered to Annabella's building. Acknowledging this, he glanced over into the backseat and grabbed the straps of his duffle bag, lying it down onto the front passenger seat. Once the vans had past him, Tristan pulled over quickly and grabbed the duffle bag. Hurriedly, he hopped out of the Explorer and made his way towards the garage's entrance. Peering from around the corner from where he was on his bending knees, he saw the security guard in the booth. He had just pressed the button that lifted the arm that allowed the UPS vans access to the garage.

Tristan pulled out a bamboo stick and two darts stained with a sedative, sliding them into the hollow ending of the stick. Lifting the bamboo stick up, he shut one eyelid and took aim at his target. His cheeks swelled up with his hot breath and he blew into the end of the stick twice. Flashes appeared at the opposite end of the bamboo stick. The first dart struck the security guard in the neck and he yelped. Wincing, he grabbed the dart and pulled it out, looking at it strangely. Before he knew it a second dart struck him high in the chest. Clenching his teeth, he dropped the dart and pulled out the second one. He looked at it and found spots appearing before his eyes. His eyebrows rose and fell repeatedly and his pupils rolled into the back of his head. He released the second dart and dropped to his knees, slamming face first onto the surface. The impact from the fall busted his mouth and bloodied his grill. Eyelids shut, mouth open, his nostrils flared as he snored asleep.

Seeing that he'd taken out the security guard, Tristan made his way over in his direction in a hurry. He looked at the dispatched guard as he made his way past him en route to the vans. Seeing the enormous vehicles ahead, he ran forward and leaped up. Having grabbed a hold of the last van, he looked over his shoulder to see the scenery behind him growing smaller and smaller the further he was driven away. Turning back around, he hugged the corner of the van and placed the side of his face against it. He stood still as he was driven further down inside the bowels of the building. The tunnel that he was going inside grew darker and darker the further the van drove down into it. It wasn't long before the lighting from the background had vanished and Tristan found himself in darkness. Looking around the corner of the van, the Dominican saw a large metal shutter ahead. There was a buzzing sound and the shutter contracted into the ceiling, revealing an enormous storage space.

The UPS vans rolled inside of the storage space, which was occupied by several boxes of varies sizes from different companies. The space was well lit, allowing its occupants to see everything surrounding them. Tristan narrowed his eyelids under the intense rays of the ceiling lights. Hopping down from the van, he removed his duffle bag and slid it underneath the vehicle. Afterwards, he crawled upon the roof of the van he'd hitched a ride on. He looked around at the rest of the vans that had entered along with him, unsheathing the black escrima sticks that were in the placement on his back. He listened as the doors of the UPS vans popped open and its occupants jumped out, talking among one another as they slipped on gloves, preparing to remove the boxes that the drugs were stashed inside of.

Figuring that now was as good of a time as any; Tristan ran forward and flipped off of the roof of the van. Looking down, he saw the top of one of the drivers' heads, appearing to grow closer as he was hurling down towards it. The weight of his body upon the driver's head snapped his neck instantly, placing it at a funny angle. Upon hearing the snap of his target's neck bone, Tristan flipped forward and brought the heel of his boot down on one of the delivery guys' shoulders. He howled out in pain feeling his shoulder being dislocated. His howling was quickly halted when his attacker cracked him across the skull with one of his escrima sticks. The force behind the blow caused blood to spill out of his scalp and down his forehead. With him out of the fight, Tristan twisted around and kicked another one of the delivery men across the chin, sending him flying off to the side. The Dominican then brought his other escrima stick around, cracking another one of the men across the lower half of his face. The assault dislocated the man's bottom jaw and left him biting to the left, teeth chattering. His eyes were bugged as he fell to the floor. Tristan hit the floor with the man, but sprung right back upon his booted feet. He engaged another one of the delivery men. He swung one of his sticks down upon his shoulder blade and he screamed in agony. The next hit he felt was at his elbow which broke it. The third hit fractures his kneecap and a fourth shattered his collar bone. A solid kick to the mid section sent him flying backwards into a stack of boxes. He hit the floor with the boxes tumbling down on him.

Tristan whipped his head back around to find a lone delivery man. This son of a bitch was so big that he looked like he belonged on someone's football field. He had a huge head and a body the size of a goddamn dump truck. The big man cracked his knuckles and smiled wickedly, licking his lips. Right then, he charged forward, swinging haymakers at Tristan. Although he was a giant, he was fast but not faster than his opponent. The Dominican ducked and dodged all of his advances swiftly, attacking his ribcage and his limbs with his trusty sticks. The giant winced and scowled, but kept trying to knock his foe's head off his fucking shoulders. No matter how fast he moved, the slender man was just that much faster, managing to avoid him.

Finally, the big man stopped, breathing hard as hell. He stood before his opponent with hooded eyes, chest jumping up and down from his quick movements. He was so exhausted that he couldn't throw another punch, which left him at the Dominican's mercy. Before he could bat an eyelash, the big man was kicked in the balls. The pain that shot through his southern region crossed his eyes and made him grab his family jewels. Tristan blew his victim's cap from off of his head and it fell to the floor. He followed up by spreading his arms apart and swinging his sticks inward, en route to either side of the big man's skull. The impact of the sticks sent one of his eyeballs flying from out of his head and deflecting off of Tristan's shirt. The other eyeball was left bulging out of its socket. Blood ran in small streams from out of the giant's eyes and ears. On his knees with an opened mouth, he slightly shook and then fell over on his side dead.

Still holding the sticks in his hands, Tristan turned around in a circle looking at all of the men that he had dispatched on his own. The ones that weren't dead were bawling in agony on the floor. Acknowledging this, he sheathed the sticks on his back and crept to the back of the van that he'd stashed his duffle bag underneath. He removed some zip-cuffs and restrained the men that were still alive. Afterwards, he gagged their mouths so that they couldn't scream for help. Next, he opened the double doors of all of the UPS vans. He withdrew a bowie knife and made his way over to the last van. Opening its double doors, he climbed inside and pulled out a small flashlight, which he used to shine on the cargo inside. The bright orb that the flashlight illuminated swept across the cardboard boxes labeled fragile. Sticking the small flashlight between his teeth, he made his way over to the boxes and cut it open with his knife. Pulling down the flap that he'd made out of the box with his knife caused the stuffing to come pouring down on the vehicle's floor. Tristan sheathed his knife and took out the colorful vase that he found inside. Taking it by one hand, he smashed it against the wall of the van and it shattered. There was a thud as something fell to the floor. He dropped what was left of the vase in his hand and shined his flashlight on what had fallen from the breakage. It was then that he found a kilo of cocaine wrapped up in clear plastic.

Having made sure that the drugs were housed inside of the boxes, Tristan killed the illumination of the flashlight and hurried out of the van. He removed the placement on his back that held his sticks and set it aside on the floor. He then looped the strap of his duffle bag over his shoulders and went around to all of the vans, placing an explosive device on them. Once he was done, he pulled out the detonator to the explosives and stashed it on him. After throwing the duffle bag aside he fled to the lone door that allowed individuals to enter the storage space. He appeared as a silhouette as he stood in the doorway of the dark hall, the light of the storage space shining on his back. He looked down the hallway for anyone that may be patrolling the building, knowing that there was definitely security on deck. That he was sure of. Hell, somebody had to guard that cocaine.

Tristan looked to his left and saw a light that outlined the men's restroom door, golden light making it look like a burning rectangle set against darkness. At that moment he heard a toilet flushing and placed his back against the wall, slowly creeping towards the men's restroom door. As soon as he reached the door it was being pulled open by a man dressed in an ensemble that resembled a S.W.A.T team member's uniform.

This nasty mothafucka didn't even wash his hands, Tristan thought before he swung out in the doorway, surprising homeboy that had just finished flushing the toilet. He chopped him in his throat and he grabbed his neck. He poked him in his eyes and he yelped, smacking his gloved hands over his face. Swiftly, Tristan grabbed him by the back of the neck and slammed him face first into the restroom's wall, knocking him out cold. The nigga fell out on the floor, palms up and boots pointed to the ceiling. Tristan, holding the restroom door open, looked up and down the corridor before stepping inside. He stepped over the nigga that he'd knocked out cold and looked down at him, checking the pulse in his neck to make sure he hadn't killed his ass. When he checked his pulse he winced. Standing back up, he lifted his shirt and took a look at the wound he'd gotten from being shot with an arrow. There was gauze and bandages wrapped around it. At the center of the bandages there was blood that had soaked through them. His wound was giving him hell since the pain killas had worn off, but he had to press on if he was going to get the job done.

Tristan removed his gear and equipment. He then put on the clothing and gear of the man that he'd knocked out cold. Afterwards, he drugged homeboy into a stall and sat him down on the commode, shutting the door behind him. Once he was done, he made his way for the exit door. As soon as he stepped out he found someone else there that was dressed exactly like him, except he was wearing a scowl on his face. Seeing this expression, the Dominican went to pull his handgun from its holster and put one in his brain, but what he said next stopped him.

"You okay in here, Levon? I thought I heard a fall." he said concerned.

"Yeah," Tristan replied in a disguised voice. "I slipped and fell. Goddamn janitor didn't put the wet floor sign up. I nearly broke my fucking neck."

"Fuckin' asshole, come on," he placed his gloved hand on his shoulder and ushered him out of the restroom. At that precise moment they heard a rumbling upstairs and then gunfire. They exchanged glances and took off running down the hallway. The leading man radioed the rest of the security team to meet them on the 20th floor. Having done this, he and Tristan took their MP-5s into both hands and hauled ass to the elevators. The rest of the security team boarded the elevator beside theirs.

***

Eureka scaled up the side of a twenty story building. Making it to the ledge, she pulled herself upon it and took in her surroundings. There was bird shit and pigeons occupying the ledge. As she moved forth, the pigeons flew off and left feathers floating around in the air. Eureka stopped in her tracks, spotting the surveillance cameras around the tenement. Fuck, she cursed to herself, she didn't count on the building being equipped with security cameras. They were located at her front and back. They turned around and zoomed in on her. With blinding speed, she threw silver ninja stars. They spun around fast through the air twisting and turning, slicing through the cords that allowed them to operate. The surveillance camera at her rear fell and deflected off the side of the building, while the other fell straight down. With the cameras taken care of, Eureka crept forward like a cat burglar. Making it to the window that she believed belong to her target, she pulled out a tool that was specifically used to cut glass; a suction cup was attached below it. Placing the tool against the window, she turned the cutter and made a complete circle. Next, she pressed the suction cup against the glass and gripped the handle of it. With two good tugs, she removed the glass that she'd cut out and sat it down on the ledge. Snaking her hand inside of the hole she created, she grasped the brass door handle and opened it. When she made her way inside, she found Annabella staring up at a portrait of her and her father, casually sipping champagne.

Suddenly, Annabella dropped the flute at her feet and its contents spilled on the floor. Swiftly, she whipped around and pointed a chrome shotgun at Eureka, smiling devilishly. Eureka's eyelids stretched wide open and she gasped. The shotgun jerked violently and flames roared out of its barrel. The impact from the pellets sent Eureka's ass hurling backwards across the office, flipping over the desk and landing on her stomach. Gritting in pain, she lifted her head up and looked up at Annabella, who was strolling in her direction, smoking shotgun held at her side.

"Now, I know your little ass didn't think you were gonna come breaking into my shit and knock me off that easily, did you? Huh, bitch?" she hauled off and kicked Eureka hard as shit in her ribs, slightly lifting her off of the carpet. She then stomped her in the back and head. "Who sent chu, huh? What's the mothafucka's name? I wanna know." Annabella snatched the disguise off of Eureka's head and tilted her head to the side, looking at her enemy's face. "Humph, I know you. You were there when homeboy killed my father. Yeah, I remember you, bitch. I sent a hitta at that bitch made ass nigga of yours. So, while my hit-man is taking care of your little boyfriend, I'll be taking care of you." Annabella unsheathed Eureka's katana and admired it, twisting it from side to side. A gleam swept up the length of the lethal weapon and it twinkled at its tip. Its illumination shined on her face and she cracked a grin, marveling the beautifully crafted sword.

Annabella walked over to a katana that was hung upon her wall. It sat above another katana, their handles facing in the opposite directions. She yanked the sword from its holding place and brought it around, holding it up. She held tight to this sword and threw the other. The bladed weapon went high up into the air, spinning around so fast that it looked like a helicopter propeller. It went flying downwards and landed into its rightful owner's palm. Eureka curled her fingers around the handle of the katana and brought it down from the air, flipping it over in her palm. She did a lot of fancy maneuvers with the katana, bringing it around her back and swinging it around to the front of her. She got into a martial arts fighting stance and brought the katana up at her shoulders. The light bulb from the ceiling kissed off of the katana and it illuminated her face. Her eyebrows arched and wrinkles formed around her nose.

Annabella smiled satanically and licked her lips. She then kicked off her high heels and did fancy moves with her sword, like her foe. She could tell that Eureka was impressed with her skills. This made her smile that much harder.

"Unh huh, I bet you thought that I was just some uppity ass trust fund baby, born with a silver spoon in her mouth, fooled you." She flipped her katana around her back and caught it. Bringing it back around, she slid into formation.

"Aaaaaaaah!" Eureka took off at Annabella.

"Raaaaaaah!" Annabella took off right after her.

In the blink of an eye, Eureka and Annabella went charging at one another, swinging their katanas with all they had. The clashing of sharp metal resonated throughout the office and sparks flew every which way. Hatred and determination was plastered on the ladies faces and beads of sweat oozed from out of their pores and ran down their faces. The fight was evenly matched. They went kick for kick, punch for punch and swing for swing. There was grunting, blood and sweat flying through the air. Before either of them knew it, their clothing had tears in it and they were bleeding badly. Eureka had come out on the losing end. She found herself feeling faint and weak but she pushed herself, determined to be the last woman standing.

Bwap! Wap! Wop!

Annabella gave her two swift kicks across the face and followed up with a slug to the jaw, sending spit flying. Her counter move was a hard kick to the midsection. The force behind the impact slammed her against the window and made pigeons fly away, leaving feathers drifting in the air. Eureka turned around facing the glass wincing, still holding her sword. Hearing hurried footsteps behind her; she peeled her eyelids open and saw Annabella leaping into the air. Her eyes lit up and she moved out of the way at the last minute.

Thoom!

The heel of Annabella's pump cracked the glass into a cobweb and embedded its self. She tried yanking her foot back several times but her shoe wouldn't budge. Seeing her chance to attack, Eureka sprung forth and cracked her in the jaw, sending spittle and specks of blood flying. The blow snatched her out of her pump, leaving it lodged in the window and her falling to the floor. Still holding her sword, she flipped over and came back up. She lifted her katana and heaved, blood dripping from her nostrils and chin. Little momma looked really pissed off now.

Eureka stood with a smirk on her face and her blade at her side, amused at her hurting of her enemy. She took the time to tear strips from off of her clothing and tie them around different parts of her body to slow her bleeding. She then spit off to the side and lifted her sword for battle. She and Annabella stared one another down intensely, blood and sweat dripping from off of them both. The only thing that could be heard inside of the office was their heavy breathing. The ladies were beat but this battle of theirs wouldn't come to a close until one of them was standing victorious.

Within the blink of an eye, Eureka and Annabella took off at one another. They connected with swings of their katanas, weapons loudly clashing inside of the office. They drew their swords back and swung again and again and again, sending sparks flying. The fighting got so intense that sweat poured down their forms and they found themselves growing hot and dehydrated. Still, they tried to take one another's heads off and put their beef to bed once and for all.

Claaannnng!

The foes swords met loud and hard, sound resonating throughout the office once again. They mad dogged each other, pushing their blades against one another, gritting. Their nostrils flared and they breathed hard, spit oozing out of the corners of their mouths. Suddenly, Eureka kneed Annabella in her stomach, doubling her over. She followed up with a straight kick to the face that lifted her chin. A final kick to the neck threw her to the side, where she landed hard and dropped her katana. Wincing, she looked around and located the chrome shotgun that she's shot Eureka with earlier. Smiling satanically, she grabbed the shotgun and whipped around. By the time that she did, Eureka was already zig zagging around the office trying not to get hit.

"I got cho black ass now, you little bitch!" Annabella pointed her shotgun at the fleeing Eureka and pulled the trigger. The powerful weapon jerked violently in her hands when it spat flames, exploding a vase across the office. The blast missed Eureka by a foot. This didn't deter Annabella though. Nah, she kept her shotgun following her and blasting at her, steadily missing her and exploded or knocking the stuffing out of some piece of furniture. Seeing the wall before her, Eureka ran up the wall and did a back flip. Just as her feet left the wall, it exploded with a large hole having taken a blast from Annabella's shotgun. Still in motion in the air, Eureka swiftly pulled a .32 from the small of her back and stabbed her sword in the floor. Standing balanced on the katana in the air, she parted her legs which made her look like the letter Y and turned to Annabella. She scowled and brought her body around to face her, pointing her small caliber gun at her. She pulled the trigger rapidly, narrowing her eyelids with each shot that spat from the weapon. With each empty shell casing that flew, a bullet entered Annabella's body. Her face contracted more and more with each bullet that she took, bloodying her white business suit. She fell back against the floor dead, eyes wide and mouth ajar. Eureka was still balancing herself on the kilt of the sword, pointing her smoking gun and forming the letter Y. A moment later, she came down on the floor and snatched her katana from where it was stuck. Cautiously, she approached her kill, chest rising and falling with ease. Her body swayed from left to right, one hand holding her katana and the other holding her .32. Stopping before her victim, she kneeled down and sat the sword aside. Taking two fingers, she placed them on an area of her neck to check her pulse. There wasn't any. Acknowledging that homegirl had expired, Eureka took a deep breath. She then picked up her sword and stood to her feet. As soon as she did, the double doors of Annabella's office came flying inward. In the doorway, a dozen men dressed up like S.W.A.T team members stood. They had MP-5s with infrared lasers pointed at the front of her.

Eureka's head snapped from left to right; she couldn't believe that there were so many men standing before her. Looking down, she saw that she was covered in what looked like one thousand infrared laser dots from the men's automatic weapons. Right then, her adrenaline began pumping crazily and her blood raced throughout her body. Every vein on her body appeared and her heart thudded, sounding inside of her ears. A hateful expression switched places with the one of shock occupying her face. She scowled and squared her jaws, causing them to pulsate. She lifted her sword and her .32, prepared to die fighting.

"Drop your weapons!" the shortest and thickest of the men ordered.

"Eat shit!" Eureka spat back.

"I said, 'drop your weapons!'"

"And I said, 'eat shiiiit!'" she roared back again, spittle jumping off her lips.

"Fiiiire!"

With the order given, the men went to pull their triggers.

Blatatatatatatat!

Blatatatatatatat!

Blatatatatatatat!

Blood splattered in Eureka's face as she hollered aloud. Hot lead flew in and out of warm flesh; there were screams so loud that they threatened to burst her eardrums. When she peeled her eyelids back open, she bared witness to the men that had their MP-5s trained on her being cut down from behind. They fell over in ones and twos, being torn apart by embers. Their screams and hollers filled the air as they met with their deaths. A confused expressed crossed Eureka's face, seeing it all happen before her eyes. She used the hand that she held her sword with to wipe the blood splatter from off her face. When she did this, there were only two of the men left but she couldn't see who it was that was opening fire on them. The men fell dead to the floor, leaving one man standing holding smoking MP-5s. He was dressed up in the same S.W.A.T gear like the men that he had laid out, but Eureka couldn't make out his face due to the security cap on his head and the neoprene mask covering the lower half of his face. Behind the man holding the MP-5s were two more men dressed exactly like him. They lay at a funny angle with their necks snapped. Eureka gathered that he had broken their necks and taken their weapons, which he'd used to unleash hell on their comrades.

"Who are you?" Eureka asked.

It was then that homeboy tossed the empty MP-5s aside and pulled the neoprene mask from the lower half of his face, revealing his identity. It was Tristan. Eureka smiled from ear to ear seeing her husband. If it hadn't been for him she would have been dead.

"You okay, baby?" he questioned concerned.

"Yeah, now that you're here, I love you."

"I love you, too."

At that moment, a concerned expression crossed Eureka's face. Tristan's forehead dipped with lines and he looked over his shoulder, seeing more of Annabella's security team filling the hallway with MP-5s. They hurried down the corridor firing at the married couple. Tristan whipped around to his wife and pulled a handgun from the holster on his hip, taking off running towards her. Bullets whizzed over his head and all around him, cracking the window's glass in front of him. Through Eureka's eyes she saw her husband moving in slow motion. He grabbed her and told her to hold on tight. She did exactly like she was ordered. At that moment, Tristan leaped through the cobwebbed window and shattered it completely. Turning around in mid air, he pulled out some kind of black tool that fit around his hand like brass-knuckles. This was a grappling gun. At this time, Eureka was facing the ground below, seeing that they were high above the streets, in wow with all of the colorful lights in the darkness.

Tristan fired the grappling gun and a line of cord spat out. The cord stabbed into the building and the couple swung out far and wide. Seeing the men in the broken out window still firing at them, Tristan pointed his handgun and popped off. His gunfire wounded some but left others dead. Holstering his weapon, he held his wife with his freehand and focused on landing. The cord he fired wrapped around the corner of the building and they disappeared from the line of fire, still hearing the MP-5s firing at them.

Blatatatatatatat! Blatatatatatatat!

Blatatatatatatat! Blatatatatatatat!

***

Tristan swung into the opening of the fourth floor of the building's parking garage. He released the grappling gun and he and Eureka went tumbling across the ground. Suddenly, they stopped, lying there wincing, hearts racing.

"You okay, baby?" Tristan asked her.

"Yeah," She nodded. "You?"

"My wound is giving me hell but I'll be okay."

Eureka rose to her feet tucking her .32 handgun at the small of her back. Holding her katana in one hand, she used the other to pull Tristan to his feet. After pulling his arm around her shoulders, she helped him walk towards the exit.

The married couple jumped back into the Ford Explorer and peeled out, Tristan pulled out the detonator and pressed the button on it. Looking into the rearview mirror at the building that they had just invaded, he saw fireballs flying out of all of the openings of the parking garage. Afterwards, he looked to his wife and dapped her up, smiling.

"Good job." Tristan complimented his wife.

"I couldn't have done it without you." Eureka told him. "Lemmie call Fear to make sure the drop went as planned." She pulled out her cellular and dialed up Fear. The cell phone rang and rang but the killa didn't answer. This caused Eureka's forehead to wrinkle.

Seeing the concern on his wife's face, Tristan said, "What's up?"

"He's not answering." She replied and dialed him up again.

Fear's cellular rang and rang.

Chapter Eight

Fear pulled up to the address of the residence that he was given. He murdered the headlights and engine of his vehicle and hopped out, slamming the door shut behind him. He took a gander at his surroundings, and couldn't believe the condition that the estate was in. He wondered why the place hadn't been torn down and replaced by some other tenement. That was the least of his concerns though. His mind was on getting his son back in one piece. For him that was of the utmost of importance.

Taking a deep breath, Fear took one step forward and heard several loud clicks. Right after, he was blinded by several bright, white orbs. The rays illuminating him were so intense that he threw up his arms and narrowed his eyelids trying to peer beyond them.

"Remove any weapons on ya person and toss dem aside…now." He heard a voice that seemed to have come from everywhere at once. It was loud and powerful. And if he didn't know any better he would have sworn up and down that it came from God Almighty.

With the order given, Fear removed the weapons hidden on him and tossed them aside. It appeared as if he had one thousand knives and guns on him that where stashed in places that even the naked eye couldn't see.

"Okay. I'm clean." Fear told him, holding up his hands and doing a 360 degree turn. As of now he was in a Kevlar bulletproof vest, cargo pants and combat boots, laced up tightly.

"If ya enter dis domain wit so much as a fuckin' safety pin, I'm goin' ta slit dis liddle bastard's throat from ear ta ear. I'm warnin' ya now, so don't say dat I didn't lata."

With that said, Fear pulled the small .22 from out of his boot and the two six inch blades secured under his pants legs, tossing them to the side.

"Thank you. Please, make ya way ta da door."

"No way, asshole, you want me? Well, you got me. You let the kid go and then I'll come waltzing in."

"Oh, really?"

"You bet cha, sweet ass." Fear hawked up a nasty glob and spat it off to the side.

"Second window to the left, please."

Fear looked to where he was told and found Kingston there. His face was mashed up against the glass and a machete was pressed up against his throat. His young eyes were stretched wide open and his mouth was ajar, pupils moving about wondering what was about to happen. He wanted to swallow the lump of nervousness in his throat but the risk of slitting it changed his mind.

"Touch 'em and I'll…"

"Shut da fuck up!" Julian roared angrily. "If I was ta slit dis liddle muddafucka's jugular, ya wouldn't be able ta do shit but watch 'em bleed out. Now, do as I said or prepare ta tell his motha about his tragic death."

"You got it, big dawg. You're the boss!" Fear's face balled up in anger.

"I thought you'd see things my way, Mr. Fear." Julian pulled Kingston away from the window. Not long after, the front door's knob clicked as it was turned and then the door swung open. Fear took a deep breath, looked down for a second, and then made his way towards the door. As soon as he crossed the threshold, the door slammed shut behind him. His head snapped over his shoulder and then he turned back around. He found Kingston standing on the tips of his sneakers on a wobbly wooden chair, a noose tied around his neck, wrists tied behind his back. The rope was so tight around his throat that the meat of his neck bulged around it. His eyes were wide open and teary, beads of sweat oozing out of his pores. The youth looked to be struggling to keep his balance. The wrong movement and he'd hang himself.

Son of a bitch, he's just a kid, Fear's eyebrows lowered and he clenched his jaws, showcasing the muscles in his face.

"I know wut ya thinkin'," Julian's voice rang out from the darkness and caused Fear to look in its direction. He narrowed his eyelids but he couldn't seem to see him, but then he saw something moving in the shadows, strolling out of the darkness. "Dat son of a bitch, he's just a kid. I had a kid once. Yes, I said once. Dis was before someone murdered him and my wife in cold blood. From dat day forth I knew dat if I wanted to be triumphant in dis game of death, then I'd have ta be just as ruthless as my enemies, or I'd become their food. You're a killa, much like me, I'm sure you'd agree."

"I'd agree," Fear's eyes cut to Kingston; he was sweating more and that chair he was on seemed to be rocking harder. He didn't know how much longer the boy could keep his balance, which meant he had to put an end to the situation fast. "I have a set of rules for myself though; no children or innocent people are to be killed on my jobs. And should I break any of those rules, I will punish myself. Other killas, rapists, drug dealers, pimps, crooked cops, shady politicians, any of them mothafuckaz can get it for the right price, 'cause they're in the game, just like you and me. You feel me, family?"

"Yeah, I feel ya," Julian nodded, standing a few feet away from Fear. He cracked a sinister grin and slightly angled his head. The kingpin turned hit-man sized him up, taking in his appearance from head to toe. To him, homeboy looked like a super villain straight off the cover of a Marvel comic in that getup that he was wearing, especially with all of those weapons attached to him. What was most noticeable to him was that mechanism on his wrist that was capable of firing a small arrow.

"Glad ya could make it ta ya funeral, chap." The corner of Julian's lips curled up in an evil smirk. He then pointed his Desert Eagle straight at Fear's chest. The shorter man didn't even flinch in the face of danger. Nah, wasn't any bitch in his blood. Homie's eyebrows sloped and he squared his jaws, veins bulging at his temples.

"I never took you for a man for an easy victory," Fear told him straight up.

"Wut do ya mean?" Julian raised an eyebrow.

"If you're a hitta then you done yo' homework on me, so that means you know what life I'm 'bout." He waited for what he had said to settle in his mind before he continued on. "You know I'm one of the best in this game of death. Seeing as how you fancy yourself as the best there is, I'd think you'd want to find out how you measured up." Fear looked at Julian as he held his gun on him. His pupils were at the corners of his eyes as he thought about what had just been said to him. This made Fear crack a barely visible smirk because he knew he got the nigga'z mental wheels turning. All he had to do now was hope that homeboy went for the bait on the line that he'd just thrown out.

"Ya right. I wanted a piece of ya eva since I read your resume," Julian tossed his Desert Eagle aside. Right after, Fear charged at him, screaming at the top of his lungs, veins bulging all over his head and body. Swiftly, he leaped high into the air and kicked Julian hard as shit in the head. The blow sent him stumbling backwards in a hurry. He didn't fall, so the killa stayed on his ass, like stink on shit. His fists came in flurries, knuckles slamming hard into his face and busting him up. When Julian went to fall, Fear gave him a rib shot that caused him to wince. He followed up with a punch to the opposite side of his ribcage. He finished him off with an uppercut, throwing his head back and sending a mist of blood into the air. Again, Julian stumbled back in a hurry. He was about to fall, but he righted himself and went after Fear. Fear recovered his formation and blocked all of the punches and kicks that came at him. He moved like he knew when his opponent was going to attack. Then he got the surprise of a lifetime, the UK assassin clapped his ears and set off an eerie siren inside of his head. Grimacing, he staggered backwards with his eyes bulging, holding his ears. Julian didn't let up on him though. Fuck showing mercy. The UK assassin tore into his midsection and made him double over. Julian grabbed him in a one arm headlock and flipped him over on his back. He landed on his back hard, gritting. He got stomped in his stomach, which made him howl in pain, holding his torso. Julian moved around him, kicking and stomping his ass. Flexing his fingers, he grabbed him by the back of his neck and grasped one of his legs. He then placed him on the back of his neck, putting him in Lex Luger's Torture Rack. Fear hollered out in pain, hearing his bones cracking and threatening to break. Having grown tired of bending up his enemy, the British executioner took him off his neck and slammed him on his back. He lay there for a second bawling and holding his sides. Julian walked around him, bending his neck from left to right and flexing his biceps.

"Dis is wut chu wanted, right, bruvh?" he talked that shit to him, knowing that he had the upper hand. "What is it dat ya call yourself again? Awww, dat's it, Fear, right? Well, Mr. Fear, I really don't see wut da big fuss is about you. I'm sorely disappointed, not impressed in da least bit." without warning, he kicked Fear in the jaw and he landed hard on his chin, looking like he was planking. The UK assassin then grabbed him by his ankle and swung him around and around, turning them into one big human tornado. They were going so fast that Fear thought the room was spinning. Before he knew it, Julian released his ankle and he went flying across the decrepit living room. He went through a wall, creating a big ass hole and causing dust to go up in the air.

"Liddle man came ta play a big boy's game, huh? I'm afraid you've gotten too big fa ya britches, ma boy." Julian kept on talking shit as he casually strolled over to the hole he created with Fear's body. All was quiet, besides the squeaking of the wooden chair that Kingston was struggling to keep his balance on. The little nigga'z eyelids were squeezed shut and he was gritting, fighting to keep his life. Julian glanced over in his direction, seeing him struggling upon the chair. "Liddle bruvh, allow me to help ya out…you can't keep death waitin' ya know?" he snatched a small knife from the small of his back and flipped it over in his palm. Turning back towards the hole he made in the wall and steadily walking towards it, he threw the knife at the chair. The blade spun around so fast that it looked like a mini Frisbee hurling through the air. The blade cut one of the chair's legs in half and Kingston dropped, but the noose snatched his little ass right back up. He swung from left to right, legs thrashing around. Veins bulged at his temples and forehead. He squeezed his eyelids shut and gritted. When he peeled his eyelids back open, his eyes were teary. "I'm afraid ya don't have a minute ta spare, Mr. Fear. It seems your offspring is headed to a land of make believe…" he finally looked over at Kingston since the first time he threw the small knife. The little mothafucka was gagging and choking at the mouth. "Yesssss, I'd say he'll be arriving there in da next seven minutes. Dat is, unless ya manage ta kill me in dat time frame, which I highly doubt." He stopped walking and held his arms spread apart. A smile etched across his lips. Grasping either side of the hole in the wall, Julian stuck his head inside of it and saw inside of a bedroom. A tattered mattress was on the floor beside a bent up bed rail. The nightstands and dressers were ruined. Where the entertainment center was against the wall, he could see that the TV was missing.

"It's time I shut ya big fuckin' mouth, bruvh!" Fear's voice rang out from his right, mocking his enemy's accent.

Bwamp!

Fear swung a "20 inch television set by its cord against Julian's head. The impact from the blow nearly dropped him, but he managed to regain his footing. Before he knew it the TV was slamming against his head again, he fell back against a pillar and caused debris to fall. When he looked up, Fear could see the blood running from his nostrils and ears. The nigga also had bruising and cuts all over his face. He saw double before his eyes but he managed to shake it off. He saw his enemy swinging something above his head fast, but it wasn't until his vision came into focus that he saw exactly what it was. Fear was spinning the television set above his head; it made a strange sound it was moving so fucking fast. He suddenly released it and it went flying towards Julian. The UK assassin kicked it out of his way and when he drew his leg back, Fear was charging at him. The killa leaped up at him and cocked his fist back.

Bwap!

He cracked him in the jaw and sent a spray of blood into the air. Coming down on his knees, he came back up warming up his ribcage with punches. The British executioner went to grab him and he smacked his hand down, giving him an uppercut. Afterwards, he tackled him through the pillar. The force behind the impact sent dust and chunks of the pillar spilling to the hardwood floor. Fear landed on top of Julian and rolled forward, off of him. Having seen one of his enemy's small knives, the killa snatched it up and sprung to his feet like a jack in the box. He threw the knife at Kingston's noose and collapsed to the floor, breathing hard. From where he lay he looked up at the knife spinning around like a small propeller, curving while en route to the rope. The spinning blade was about to slice the rope in half, when something sparked off of it and sent it flying off its target. Fear's eyes grew big and he gasped. Looking to where the spark had come from, the killa found Julian around on his feet. The dust on his face and shoulders made him look like he had been hit with powder. His shoulders rose and fell as he breathed huskily, holding his smoking Desert Eagle. He had just shot the small knife and sent it off course.

"Now, ya die," Julian swung his Desert Eagle around and pointed it at Fear. The killa rolled out of the way, just as the bullet went through the space on the floor that he was lying on. He then jumped to his feet and took off running, head ducked low.

Blam! Blam! Blam! Blam!

Fear moved like lightning, missing the bullets by inches. He moved from left to right in a zig zag, acting as a target that was unpredictable. Still in motion, he snatched up a stone that was the size of a baseball. Julian gripped his Desert Eagle with both hands and shut one of his eyelids, having finally gotten his enemy in his sight.

"Kiss ya ass goodbye." He said, pulling the trigger. The big gun bucked, releasing a piping hot bullet. It appeared to be moving in slow motion en route towards its target. At the last minute, Fear leaped into the air and flipped, pulling a small knife that was wedged inside of his boot. In the air, he did a kart wheel and launched the stone at the UK assassin. The British executioner was just pulling back on the trigger. The stone slammed into the side of the Desert Eagle just as it fired. The force behind the impact of the stone sent the big gun flying across the living room. Coming down, Fear sliced the rope that Kingston was dangling from. The boy crashed to the floor at the exact same time that his son did. Looking up from where he was lying, the killa saw Julian reaching to pick up his weapon. Quickly, he grabbed Kingston and fled across the living room, where he took refuge behind a pillar. The area where he was holing up was covered by shadows, so he couldn't be seen.

"Are you okay, son...I mean, King?" Fear looked down into his son's face as he lay in his arms. Tears stained his cheeks and he was gasping, rubbing the red burn that the noose had created around his neck. He cringed and breathed hard.

"I think...I think I'm gonna...I'm gonna be okay." The little nigga told him, chest rising and falling rapidly. "Who...who are you?"

"I'm an old friend of your mother's. You can call me Fear or Al."

"Did you say Al?" his forehead deepened with a line.

"Yeah, short for Alvin."

"Oh, that's what's up."

Fear peered around the corner of the pillar that he and his son were hidden behind. He saw Julian standing upright having picked up his Desert Eagle. Kingston took a look too, frowning seeing him and his father's common enemy.

"We've gotta kill 'em." Kingston's eyes bled his seriousness. This drew Fear to his attention. That's when he noticed that the boy was wearing the same expression that he was, looking exactly like him just then.

"Kill 'em?" Fear looked at him like he couldn't believe what he had just said. It tripped him out that the four year old talked in that manner.

The boy turned his gaze on him and said, "Yeah, kill 'em. That mothafucka sho' tried to kill me." He involuntarily touched his sore neck.

"Come out, come out wherever you are?" Julian called out to them, walking around the living room with his Desert Eagle hoisted at his shoulder.

"He has a gun...and we don't have jack shit."

"Forget the gun, I'm fearless." Kingston told him. "My uncle Anton taught me not to be scared of nothing or no one, not even death."

A slight smile crossed Fear's face hearing his boy talk so bravely. He reminded him a lot of himself.

"I think we should come up with a..."

"Heyyyy!" Kingston called out. A shocked Fear grabbed his arm but he snatched away and stepped out from the shadows. As soon as he revealed himself, the British executioner looked in his direction and cracked a smile.

"Well, well, well, wut have we here? I'll tell ya kid, if stupidity was money den you'd be quite wealthy. Stones da size of Cadillac's, but a twit ya definitely are. There's no contestin' dat."

"I'm not scared of you, put the gun down and we can fight. I'll kick your butt," Kingston did all kinds of martial arts moves and finished with a round house kick, landing in a fighting stance. He tilted his head downward and glared up at him, fists before his eyes. "Come get some, penis head, I got your number."

"And dis bullet's got ya name written all over it, sport." Julian pointed the deadly end of his Desert Eagle at Kingston and the little nigga didn't even flinch.

"Put the gun down and fight me, you coward," Kingston called out to him.

"Notta chance," The British executioner smiled devilishly.

Still hiding behind the pillar, Fear peeked around the corner of it and saw the UK assassin about to point his Desert Eagle at his son. His eyes bulged and he gasped, seeing his only child in immediate danger. Fear took off running as fast as he could in Kingston's direction, snatching him up and dashing off. He fled in time enough to miss the bullet that was meant for his son. He continued to run and his enemy continued to fire at his ass, missing him by inches.

Blam! Blam! Blam!

Fear dove out of the way of the last shot and landed behind the fireplace, which was at the center of the living room. He lay on the floor clutching Kingston's head and body against him. He clenched his jaws and his eyes darted around for someplace else to run, hearing the tyrant continuing to fire his weapon. Embers flew through the fireplace and exited out from the other side, spraying debris. When the gun clicked empty, Julian tossed it aside and pulled out a second one. He spun it around in his hand and grasped it

"Okay, gentlemen, I'm sick of da fuckin' games so…" he smacked his hands together and rubbed them up and down against each other. "Dis is how we're gonna play dis, ya gonna come out now and face me, or I'm gonna burn dis muddafucka ta da ground. Turn ya two chaps into Kentucky Fried Chicken, ya know?" Julian waited all of two minutes, and when they didn't come out he went through with his plan. He snatched up the red can of gasoline that he left in the corner and began splashing everything around him with it. Afterwards, he threw the gas can aside and pulled out a Zippo lighter. His thumb struck the metal ball mechanism of the lighter and a flame sprung to life, licking the air. He threw the Zippo aside and it landed on the flammable chemical, igniting a fire. Flames swept all around the mansion in what appeared to be a domino effect. Julian threw his head back and shut his eyelids, smile etched across his lips. He outstretched his hands, looking like the devil standing at the center of Hell. The flames of the fire danced all around him, illuminating his entire form.

"Time ta die," Julian whipped out a second Desert Eagle and spun it around in his palm, gripping it tightly right after. He extended his gun towards the fireplace, waiting for Fear or his boy to come out.

Go ahead and stick ya bloody head out so I can blow it off, Julian thought.

Chapter Nine

He looked like a blur he was moving so fast down the road switching lanes and blowing past other vehicles. The wind blew against him and ruffled his clothing. Every now and again he'd glance down at the holographic globe projecting from his motorcycle's console. Nearing his destination, he mentally prepared himself for what was to come ahead. Should one hair on his nephew's head have been harmed; he was going to pick his attacker apart, piece by piece.

"Hang on, King, unc is almost there." Anton said to himself.

Still holding the handlebars of his motorcycle, Anton stooped down on its seat and focused on the picturesque window coming up fast ahead. The ruined mansion shown on the black tinted visor of his helmet, grew larger and larger the closer he got to it. At the last possible moment, the young hitta jumped back from off of the bike and drew his twin .45 automatic handguns with the silencers. In midair, he watched as his motorcycle crashed through the picturesque window, shattering its glass. He pointed his bangers at the bikes gas tank and pulled the triggers excessively. The guns danced in their welder's hands as they spat fire furiously.

Choot! Choot! Choot! Choot! Choot! Choot! Choot!

***

Julian's head whipped around. His eyes widen and his mouth formed an O, seeing the motorcycle twisting in the air as it flew towards him. As soon as bullets stuck its gas tank and it exploded, he threw up his arms to shield himself. He wasn't fast enough though, because embers burned the side of his face and lodged into his right eye. He screamed to the heaven's feeling the excruciating pain. His mouth was stretched open so wide that every tooth in his grill and his tongue could be seen. The impact from the blast slammed him into a pillar, which cracked in half. He landed on his back, constantly screaming and holding his injured eye. Before he knew it the upper half of the pillar was falling forward. Seeing this, he hurried turned over on his hands. He was about to get up and take off running, but the pillar came crashing down on his back, pinning him to the floor. Eyelids squeezed shut, jaws squared, he tried to push himself up from the surface but his body wouldn't cooperate. This was because his back was broken upon the impact of the pillar. He was paralyzed from the waist down. Still, he continued to claw at the floor, attempting to crawl out from under the pillar. His eyes had misted with tears he was in so much mothafucking pain. Having grown exhausted, he stopped his struggling and looked ahead. Breathing hard, he caused debris to fly up into the air, like a powdery substance. His family appeared before his eyes, one by one. First there was his son, J.J, and next was his beautiful wife, Monica. She stood beside her son, arm stretched over his shoulders as they walked towards Julian, smiling.

"Hey, baby, we missed you," Monica smiled.

"Hey, dad, I missed you." J. J smiled.

"Oh, Christ," Julian's eyes pooled with tears instantly and his bottom lip trembled uncontrollably. "I've missed ya. I've missed ya so, so much." He took the time to sniffle and went on to talk. "I love ya both, and I can't wait ta be reunited with ya both." Wetness flooded his cheeks and he sniffled again, wiping his nose with the back of his fist.

"We love ya too, sweetheart, and we're here now, are ya ready ta come home withus?"

"Yes, I'd like dat…I'd like dat very, very much," he got choked up and more teardrops fell.

"Well, come on, come home wit us, honey," she motioned him over, wearing a jovial expression on her face.

"I'll come along, but not right now," he wiped his wet cheeks with the back of his fist. "I've got some unfinished business ta attend ta. I'll catch up once I tidy up here." Julian focused his attention on Fear and Anton.

***

Anton landed on his bending knees, chest rising and falling as he breathed, .45s held at his sides. He slowly rose to his feet, smoke wafting from the barrels of his identical weapons as he stood erect. He strolled inside of the mansion, focused on Julian King. The British assassin was out of commission and at his mercy. There was crackling and popping all around, the golden orange flames of the fire were alive and licking at the air. The fire illuminated Anton's form and shone on his helmet's visors. He tossed his .45s aside and pulled off his helmet, throwing it to the sidelines. He called out to his nephew. Hearing movement at his right, he looked to see a joyful Kingston come running towards him from around the pillar. The young hitta kneeled to the floor and embraced the boy, smile stitching across his baby face.

"You okay, lil' dude?" Anton asked, holding him at arm's length.

"I'll be fine." He assured him.

Anton's face twisted and he narrowed his eyelids, peering closely at the rope burn around the boy's neck. It looked like it hurt like hell, and he was sure that it did but Kingston wasn't complaining. He had been training the youth so he was sure that the high tolerance for pain had him feeling like it was nothing more than a sprang ankle. It was this, coupled with his teaching him that pain was all in the mind and that it was possible to block it all out. It was at that moment that Anton realized that he was grooming the boy to become the perfect killa, one even more skillful than himself.

"Did that foreign faggot try to hang you?" Anton inquired, inspecting the injury to his nephew's neck.

"Yeah, he would have killed me if it wasn't for him," the youth explained to him.

"Who?" the young hitta's forehead wrinkled.

"My friend Al, or Fear as he likes to be called," Kingston turned around and pointed to the pillar. When Anton looked he found Fear leaning up against the pillar, looking like he'd been through hell and back. Instantly, the younger killa scowled and rose to his feet. Seeing the hostile expression on his uncle's face, Kingston looked from him to the man that had saved his life that night.

"Run, King." Anton ordered his relative, eyes focused on Fear.

"What's the matter, Uncle Ant?" the boy looked between both men.

"Nothing. I wanna talk to Fear in private, so run...run as far away as you can. I'll catch up."

"I can wait for you." Kingston grabbed him by the wrist.

Anton whipped around to his sister's only son and said with authority, "King, get the fuck outta here, I'm not gonna tell yo' lil' ass again."

Anton mad dogged his nephew. The youth stared into his eyes. The boy loved and respected him. It was his respect for him that made him do as he was ordered. Looking back at Fear, he ran over and gave him an affectionate hug before running out of the mansion. He stopped at the doorway, looking between both of the men for a minute before continuing on out of the door. Something in his head told him that his uncle was going to do something more than just talk to Fear, but he wasn't going to stick around to find out. Nah, he had been given an order and he was going to follow it.

"You're excellent liar." Fear told Anton as he casually strolled over to him.

"Suck my dick!" Anton mad dogged him.

Fear scowled and his nose wrinkled up. "That'll be the last time you invite me to yo' dick, son."

"We'll see."

Froooooosh! Froooooosh!

The fire raged out of control and chunks of the ceiling fell, crashing to the floor and all around the killas as they stood facing one another. Here was the time, here was the place for it all to come to a head and be settled once and for all. They stood there mad dogging one another, jaws clenched and fists balled.

"So, this is what chu been waiting for, huh?" Fear asked of the brawl that was about to go down between them.

"For the past four years I dreamed of this day. The day where I'd leave from our battle whistling and holding your severed head under my arm."

"Hmmm," Fear's eyebrows arched further. "The kid gloves are off. You wanted to tangle with the best of the best, kid? Well, you've got 'em, champ, 'cause tonight I'm not holding back."

"That's exactly what I want, old man." Anton pulled off his mask and let it drop to the floor. Next, he removed his shoulder pads and the rest of his gear, including his utility belt. When he was done disrobing, he was left naked from the waist up. He flexed his muscles and bent his limbs, preparing himself to lock ass with one of the most feared men in the murder for hire game. Fear removed his gear and the rest of his weapons, flexing his muscles and preparing for this encounter as well.

Bwap! Crack! Thwap!

As the killas rumbled, Julian moaned and pushed the wreckage from off of his person. He rubbed the back of his head with his gloved hand and squeezed his eyelids shut, feeling the migraine that had formed. Looking ahead he saw two blurred images moving around hastily, attacking one another. He blinked his eyelids repeatedly and his vision slowly came into focus. It was Anton and Fear engaging in a heated battle that would surely be talked about for centuries.

Julian wiped the blood that had rolled down his forehead and bled into his eye. It burned like salt in an opened wound, but he ignored it, because he had a mission to complete. After arming his wrist mechanism with a small arrow, he lifted his fist and took aim at Fear. His hand moved from left to right trying to find the right moment to open fire on the seasoned executioner.

Bwap! Bop! Bwhack!

Fear cracked Anton across his face twice and kicked him in the balls, doubling him over. Once the young hitta grabbed his privates, the killa slipped behind him and wrapped his arms around his waist. With a grunt, he slammed that mothafucka on his head. Anton lay there on his back wincing, arms and legs lying flat out. Fear jumped back upon his booted feet. Not waiting for his opponent to get up, he ran over and kicked him in his ribs. This drew a howl of pain from the young hitta. Next, Anton's back and head were met with hard stomps; each stomp caused his face to wrinkle more and more in pain.

"Is this what chu wanted, lil' nigga? You come at the bull, you get the fucking horns!" He kicked him in his mouth and busted his grill, sending blood flying and red teeth trickling to the ground. He gave him one more stomp for good measure, then stepped back and gave him room to get back on his feet. His fists were before his eyes and he was in a martial arts fighting stance, ready to put that work in.

"You brought it to this, youngin', I didn't want to do this to you but yo' ass was begging for it." Fear felt bad about doing his former protégé dirty but he reasoned that he wasn't holding back, so neither would he. Only one of them would be leaving alive that night and he was going to make sure that it was him.

Anton moaned and groaned in agony. He lifted his head from off of the surface and spit out blood, pushing up from off of the floor with wobbly hands. He blinked his eyelids repeatedly, trying to gather his wits and rationalize everything. It took some time but he finally managed to get upon his booted feet. He licked the excess blood from around his mouth and spit it off to the side.

"Exactly what I wanted, my nigga…no holding back," Anton slid into a martial arts fighting stance, making his fingers into the shapes of claws. He and his former teacher stared one another down, chests slowly rising and falling, oxygen filling their lungs. There was the sound of rushing fire and then a chunk of the ceiling fell, crashing to the floor. Upon impact, the two combatants took off at each other, exchanging fists and kicks. Their limbs looked like flashes they were coming so mothafucking fast.

Bwap! Wap! Whock! Swhack!

The executioners blocked and avoided one another's attacks, launching their own. Anton ducked two wild swings and a sweep kick from Fear, jumping over his leg. When he came back down, he gave him two to the torso and two to the face. A powerful kick to the mid section sent the killa staggering back in a hurry, slamming up against one of the pillars and causing debris to fall. When Fear shook off his daze, he heard a battle cry rip through the air. He looked up just in time to see Anton flying into his torso with a kick. The blow knocked the wind out of him. The young killa quickly followed up with a punch to his jaw, as he came down from the flying kick. When he landed to the surface, he came back up and launched what looked like one thousand punches to Fear's body. When he went to deliver the knockout punch, the killa caught it. He threw another one and he caught that one as well. Anton tried to kick him in the balls and he caught his leg midway. Anton looked down at Fear's knees incasing his leg and then back up into his face. He got the surprise of his life when Fear head butted him. The force from the impact sent him staggering back, seeing stars and moons before his eyes.

Anton righted himself before his back could meet the floor. Shaking off his daze, he touched the lower half of his face and his fingers came away bloody. That's when he realized that his nose was broken and blood had drenched his mouth and chin. Grabbing his nose bone, he snapped it back into place. Afterwards, he got into a martial arts fighting stance again. Once again, he and his mentor stared one another down. The ruined mansion was hot and humid. Glowing embers floated through the air from the burning wood that made up the residence. The smell of burning wood filled the air, making it hard for the combatants to breathe. The heated glass of the windows cracked and then imploded.

"Aaaaaah!" Anton charged at Fear.

"Aaaaaah!" Fear charge at him.

The killa ducked and dodged the attack that his rival launched, nearly getting injured. Fear ducked Anton's claw attack, but when he came back up, he was slashed across the both cheeks and his chest. He started bleeding instantly, blood running down his face and chest. He glanced down at his wound, and that's when Anton saw his chance to put their fight to an end. Feeling movement heading his way, Fear looked up in time to see Anton's right, clawed hand coming at his chest. Swiftly, he grabbed him by his wrist and twisted it, making him holler aloud. Right after, the young killa was coming around with his other claw. He managed to put the tips of his fingers into Fear's left peck, causing pain.

"Grrrrrr," Fear squeezed his eyelids shut and clenched his jaws so tight that his forehead wrinkled. Spit involuntarily flew from his lips, feeling the fingers sink further into his peck. He knew that Anton intended to rip his beating heart out of his ribcage, but he'd be damned if he let him. Fuck that!

"Oooof," Anton's eyes bulged and he leaned forth from Fear punching him in the stomach. Holding the young hitta's right wrist, the killa continued to deliver blow after blow to his torso. Swiftly, he hoisted him up above his head for a while before releasing him and stepping back. Anton plummeted to the floor and hit it hard, sending dust up into the air. Afterwards, Fear picked him up and hoisted him over his shoulders. Looping his arm around his neck and the other around his right leg, he went charging forward. His eyes were focused on the pillar in front of him. It seemed to get closer and closer the harder and faster that he ran toward it.

Boom!

Fear slammed him against the pillar and dust sprayed from it. Anton winced more and more as he continued to slam him into it, repeatedly. Then, all of a sudden, the killa dropped him and he hit the surface with a thud, defeated. He then placed his boot on his back and looked down at him, wiping his bloody lip with the back of his fist.

"You're good, kid, you're just not good enough," Fear told his former student. Unbeknownst to him, Anton's eyelids fluttered open and he saw Julian taking aim at Fear with the mechanical weapon attached to his wrist that fires arrows. The young hitta's eyelids stretched wide open when he saw the UK assassin smile evilly, seeing that he had Fear locked in his weapon's sight. The British executioner squeezed down on the firing button. The arrow flew across the living room moving in what appeared to be slow motion, en route to its intended target. Having taken note of this, Anton leaped from where he was and tackled Fear to the floor. Dust flew up from the floorboards due to the impact of their fall. The arrow flew right past them, missing Fear by a hair and stabbing into a pillar far across the room.

Anton lifted his head off Fear and went to work on his face, busting his shit up. Specks of blood clung to his face, punches coming one after the other. Once he stopped Fear's face was swollen and bloody, he looked like he was going to need reconstructive surgery if he was ever going to look like himself again. Anton looked at him like he was an odd painting. He then looked at his bloody knuckles, chest expanding and shrinking with every breath that he took.

"I didn't come this far to let some nigga in a faggot ass Halloween costume kill you. Nah, mothafucka, that honor belongs to me." Anton got upon his feet and looked around. Spotting a large rock across the room, he picked it up. It was warm from the fire. Sluggishly, he walked over to Julian, who looked like he was on the brink of death. The UK assassin stared up at him with narrowed eyelids, breathing shallowly. "You came at my nephew? My family, mothafucka? That's yo' ass, bitch!" Anton slammed the rock into his head, hearing his skull crack and ooze with blood. Grunting, he slammed it again and again and again, caving that mothafucka's skull in. Specks of blood splashed on his upper body and clothing, as he continued to slam the rock into his head. The rock was stained burgundy once he was finally finished with him. He tossed the rock aside and looked over his handiwork, admiring the bloody mess he'd made. Seeing the handcuffs attached to Julian's belt, he reached over and removed them from off his waist. After taking the time to spit on the corpse, he rose to his feet and staggered over to Fear, holding his side. He grabbed him by his leg and dragged him over to a radiator on the other side of the room, handcuffing him to it.

"I'm not gonna kill you, I'ma let chu burn to death in here, you piece of shit!" He kicked Fear in the side and spit on his ass. Afterwards, he looked up into the sky through the holey ceiling, talking to his late father. "Rest in peace, daddy." he crossed himself in the sign of the crucifix and walked off, making his way towards the door. As he walked away, more of the ceiling came crashing down to the floor, and then the water heater exploded. The blast sent a hacksaw, a screwdriver, a wrench, among other tools flying inside of the living room. Before long, Anton disappeared through the door, leaving a barely conscious Fear to burn alive.

The killa's eyelids fluttered open and he moaned, slowly getting upon his feet. He went to move and his wrist was snagged on something. Looking at it, he found that he was wearing a handcuff, which was attached to the radiator. He yanked and yanked on it, but that bitch wouldn't budge for anything. Grunting, he continued to yank again on the radiator causing the metals to clink, over and over again. Having grown tired, he looked around for something that he could use to free himself but he couldn't find anything.

"Fuck!" Fear cursed, realizing that he was stuck. He was sweating profusely and his body was warm. The fire was roaring all around him. He heard the glass windows imploding upstairs from the heat. The fire surrounding him was getting deathly close to him, and he found the area around him enclosing. Looking up through the boarded up window before him, he saw Anton opening the door of the vehicle that he'd drove there in. He left the door open as he kneeled down inside of the car, hot wiring it nonetheless. The automobile kicked alive and smoke roared out of its exhaust pipes. At that moment, he sat up in the driver seat and slammed the door shut. He busted a U-turn in the middle of street and stopped the vehicle, looking through the boarded up window at Fear. He sat there for a time watching him from inside of the mansion. Fear thought that maybe he was weighing the decision that he had just made, and was going to change his mind and come back for him. But he was wrong though. That mothafucka drove off, leaving his former teacher to burn to death.

"Aaahhh!" Fear threw his head back hollering, feeling the flames of the fire sizzle away the hairs of his arm and back. His head snapped to the right and he saw that the fire was too close for comfort, its glow illuminating his face. Seeing this, Fear yanked and yanked on the handcuff repeatedly. Balling up his face and clenching his jaws, he continued to try to get loose from the radiator. Realizing that his efforts to get free were useless, he stopped and took in his surroundings again. There wasn't anything around him that hadn't been engulfed by flames besides himself. He knew he'd be next.

Sweat oozed out of Fear's pores and rolled down his face and body. This was the end of the road for him. This was his fate, so he'd have to accept it. It was what it was. With that in mind, he unleashed his final hoorah.

"Aaaaaaah!" Fear threw his head back again, hollering at the top of his lungs. Veins bulged at his temples and neck.

Ka-Boom!

***

Vroooom!

Anton ripped down the street in Fear's vehicle. One hand held the steering wheel while the other adjusted the rearview mirror. He then looked into the side-view mirror, seeing the burning mansion behind him growing smaller and smaller the further he drove away.

Fuck 'em! He had it coming a long time now, Anton thought. Right after, his eyes became teary. Although he had finally taken Fear out of the game, he was still emotionally hurt. In killing him, he had taken out his friend, father figure and mentor. He hated him for having murdered his father, but at the same time he loved him. His loyalty belonged to his father though, the man that had created him. There wasn't any way he could see himself being cool with the mothafucka that whacked out his pops.

Damn, this nigga was my nephew's father too. My lil' nigga may grow up to hate me for taking his father from him. Shit is crazy.

Anton heard his cell phone ringing inside of his pocket. He whipped it out and answered it. He chopped it up for a minute and then hung up. Looking ahead, he saw Kingston running down the street. The little nigga slowed to a jog before eventually walking. It was from this that Anton knew that he was exhausted from running. He pulled up on the side of him and he whipped around. His face was balled up with anger and his fists were clenched, looking like he was ready for a fight. When he saw that it was his uncle behind the wheel, the hostility drained from his face and he un-clenched his fists.

"Uncle Anton, you made it," Kingston beamed excitedly.

"Come on, jump in," Anton motioned for his nephew to hop in the vehicle. He cracked a smile seeing Kingston run around the car en route to the front passenger seat. The little nigga opened the door and climbed in, struggling to pull his door shut. As soon as he slammed the door shut, he turned around and hugged his uncle. Anton kissed the top of his head and rubbed his hand up and down his back affectionately.

"I thought you were going to die."

"Nah, I done cheated death one thousand times. This makes one thousand and one."

Kingston smiled and looked to the backseat. His brows furrowed when he didn't see Fear there. He looked back to his uncle and said, "Where's Fear?"

Anton's eyes turned glassy and sad. He bowed his head and then he looked back up. "I'm sorry, King, but he didn't make it."

"Really?" the little nigga looked at Anton sadly and he nodded. "He…he saved my life." He looked away, not wanting his uncle to see the tears that had accumulated in his young eyes. He bowed his head and he squeezed his eyelids shut, depleting his tears. When he lifted his head, he licked his lips and took a deep breath. Seeing how hurt his nephew was, Anton hugged him again and kissed his head.

"Strap on yo' seat belt, we finna get up outta here." Anton told his nephew. Once the little nigga did as he was told, his uncle put the car into gear and drove off.

Chapter Ten

Twenty minutes later

Anton looked over to his nephew and found him drifting off to sleep; head leaned up against the front passenger side door. It wasn't long before the little nigga'z eyelids had finally shut, chest rising and falling peacefully. A smirk curled the corner of Anton's lips seeing his sister's son finally at ease and asleep. He turned his attention to the windshield and turned on the stereo, changing the channel to an Oldies station. He nodded his head to the soulful sounds of Marvin Gaye's *Let's stay together*, hand gripping the steering wheel as he gangsta leaned in the driver's seat.

Anton pulled up in the driveway of his mansion and killed the engine. He nudged his nephew who stirred awake, rubbing the corners of his eyes with his knuckles. Once the boy finally looked around and saw that he was home, a smile stretched across his youthful face. Anton smiled back weakly and ruffled his head. Hearing the locks of his front door coming undone, they looked to the porch. The door was being pulled open by Eureka, Tristan standing behind her. The young hitta took a deep breath as he took in his sister. He had to break the news to her. He expected her to be hurt by what he had to tell her but fuck it. There was no way he was going to keep this secret away from her. It would eat at him for the rest of his life.

"Mommyyyyy," Kingston's eyes lit up and he hurriedly unlocked the front passenger door. He hopped out and went charging towards his parents. The little nigga jumped right into his mother's arms. She hugged him lovingly and kissed the side of his face. Pulling back, she took a good look at him and examined his body, making sure that he wasn't wounded. Her forehead creased seeing the rope burn around his neck.

She asked him was he okay and he said no. Afterwards, she appointed her husband, who was hugging their son affectionately, to apply some ointment to the boy's neck. He gave her a nod and then kissed her before treading back up the stairs, walking inside of the mansion.

Eureka looked to the Impala just in time to see her brother hopping out and slamming the driver's door shut. He strode towards her and she took off running towards him. They wrapped themselves up in one another's arms and rocked from side to side, overjoyed to be reunited. She kissed the side of his face and looked up to the sky, thanking God for allowing her sibling to make it home in one piece. Peering over his shoulder at the Impala, she looked into the backseat. Her forehead deepened with grooves, expecting him to be there but he wasn't.

Eureka broke her brother's embrace and looked him in the eye. "Where's Fear?"

Anton shook his head, this let her know that he didn't make it. Her eyes instantly pooled with tears. Water ran down her right cheek and she wiped it away with the back of her hand. She sniffled and continued on, "Did Julian kill 'em?" she swallowed the lump of hurt that had taken form in her throat.

Anton bowed his head and shook it, saying just above a whisper, "No." he fidgeted with his hands and glanced up at his sister, not knowing how to tell her exactly what happened to her former mentor and lover.

"Then what happ…" The words died in her throat just then and her eyelids stretched wide open. She gasped and staggered backwards, both hands pressed against her heart. "No, no, no, you didn't, Anton. Please, tell me you didn't kill him." Tears flooded down her cheeks and she trembled uncontrollably. She felt her heart, her soul, her entire spirit breaking.

Anton took a deep breath and gathered the courage to look her in the eyes. "I did…I killed Fear."

"Oooooooou," she dropped down to her knees, sobbing loud and hard, her big teardrops splashing on the ground. "Oh God, no, no, no, no, Anton, he was King's father!" she rocked back and forth, hugging herself. She did this because she believed that she would fall apart, not only spiritually but mentally. The news fucked her up royally, and she wasn't sure if she'd recover.

"You right...he was King's father and Bootsy was ours. He took our father's life, so I took his," his face twisted in anger and he clenched his jaws, causing the muscles there to appear.

"What does that solve? What does that solve, huh?" Eureka's pained voice rang out in the night like gunfire in the ghetto. "It solves nothing, baby boy! Absolutely nothing! It only continues that cycle of hate and revenge. You can't see that? You murdered Fear 'cause he murdered daddy. Should King find out that you murdered his biological father he'll more than likely hate chu, and want to murder you too. Then if he succeeds and you have a child, he'll come looking to take revenge against my son." Hearing this, Anton bowed his head. He didn't say it verbally but his sister was right. There was a good chance that if Kingston found out that he murdered his father that he would come looking to take his head for it.

"Ahhaahaahaahaa, whyyyyy? God, oh, whyyyy did you let this happen?" Eureka stared up at the sky, seeing the moon and the twinkling stars sprinkled around it. Eureka bowed her head and tried her best to gather herself. She felt her ears and the back of her neck growing hot. Little momma was hot, really fucking hot. Her head snapped up and she locked eyes with her brother. Her eyebrows arched and she snarled, clutching her fists so tight that veins appeared on them. "You mothafucka, you killed my baby's fatherrrr!" she took off running full speed ahead at Anton. He had more than enough time to mount a defense but he didn't even bother. The young hitta knew that his sister needed someone to take her heartache out on and he would be perfect seeing as how he was the one that caused it.

Bwap! Bwop! Wamp!

Eureka's feet went across her brother's face quick and hard, sending blood flying through the air. Right before he could fallback, she planted her hand on the surface and kicked him underneath the chin; a mist of blood went up in the air. Anton fell to the ground hard and Eureka came down on her bending knees. Hatred was plastered across her face as she stared at her brother. A dazed expression was on his face as he attempted get upon his feet three times, bleeding at the mouth. He blinked his eyelids several times and tried to get back up again. This time he finally managed to stand erect. He wobbled from side to side and he looked high in the face but he was actually woozy.

"Fi…finish it…finish it!" Anton hollered out to Eureka, egging her to kill him off.

"Aaaaahhhh!" Eureka screamed at the top of her lungs, running at her brother. She was about to deliver the Kill-Shot, a blow that she was positive would break his fucking neck. The harder she ran the closer he seemed to be getting, before she knew it she was leaping up high into the air, legs bent underneath her. Realizing that she was about to murder her brother, the hostility drained from off of Eureka's face and the tension released from her body. Her shoulders slumped and she unclenched her fists. She landed to the ground on her bending knees and stood up, grabbing her barely conscious brother before he could meet the ground. He moaned in pain and blinked his eyelids repeatedly, like he didn't know where he was, bleeding at the mouth.

"Oh my God, baby boy, I'm sorry. I'm so sorry, I lost it, I snapped. Please…please forgive me." She cried, truly hating herself for what she had done to her younger brother. She had nearly killed him, and had she done what she'd set out to do, she would have never forgiven herself for as long as she lived.

144

Anton swallowed the blood in his grill and tasted metal. He squeezed his eyelids shut briefly and licked his lips, peeling his eyelids back open. "It's…it's okay." He wrapped his arms around her and felt her shivering, tears sliding down her face. Before he knew it he felt hot stings in his pupils, as he was attempting to cry. He wasn't emotional because the way that his sister was feeling. Nah, that wasn't it. He was this way because after finally getting his revenge he still didn't feel any better. See, Anton had assured himself that once he took out that nigga Fear that his father could finally rest in peace and he could feel at ease. Unfortunately for him this wasn't true. He felt like shit inside. His heart was still aching and he still felt bitter. The young hitta was afraid now. Why? Because if he didn't find any tranquility in completing what he deemed as the most important mission in his life, then he was most likely doomed to live as he always had…haunted.

Eureka pulled away from Anton and looked up in his eyes. "Listen, I want an entire new start for us as a family. No more secrets, no more lying. You're gonna have to tell King the truth about what happened to Fear. Tristan and I will tell him about him being his biological father."

Anton took a deep breath and looked away. Looking back, he responded, "Okay, alright, I'm gonna tell 'em."

"Thank you." Eureka nodded and continued, "Also, Tristan told me that you were teaching King how to fight, raising him to be a killa like us."

"Right," He concurred. "I was teaching him how to defend this family should I or his father perish, as well as how to operate the family business."

"Well, if you want to be in his life I'm gonna need you to give up the murder game…no more killing. Can you do that, huh? Can you do that for our family?" she looked him straight in his eyes.

There was silence as Eureka stared into her face for a while before answering, "Yeah, I can do that. I'll sell all of my cars and the motorcycle I got down there, get rid of all of my costumes, and get rid of all of the weapons from the armory. I will shut down the access panel down there as well. The Shadow will be no more."

"Good." She cupped her hands around his face and kissed him affectionately on the forehead.

Looking ahead, Anton saw Kingston standing at the front door, staring out at him. Wondering what her brother was looking at, Eureka broke her embrace from her sibling and turned around. She was just in time to see Tristan stepping behind their son and pulling the door open. They both stood there for a while staring at the sister and brother. Suddenly, Kingston took off running down the steps towards his mom. He got about three feet away before he leaped into her arms and hugged her lovingly. She shut her eyelids and smiled, rubbing her hand up and down his back soothingly. When she peeled her eyelids back open, she saw her husband still at the front door. She waved him over and he hurried down the steps as fast as he could. As soon as he reached his wife and son, he embraced them, sharing in a tender family moment. Anton stood off to the side rubbing his jaw, still feeling the aching in it from his sister's attack. Looking up from where she was hugged up with her family, Eureka grabbed her brother and pulled him closer. With that, they all had one big family hug.

There isn't anything like family.

***

Kingston and his parents sat at the kitchen table. Anton opened the refrigerator and rummaged through the shelf until he found a Yahoo, his nephew's favorite drink. Walking over to Kingston, he removed the cap and sat the bottle down before him. The boy thanked his uncle and watched as he stepped behind his mother and father. Kingston took a drink of his chocolate beverage. When he brought the bottle down from his mouth, he had a milk mustache. A frown found its way upon his face as he looked around at his family, wondering why they were all staring at him like they were.

"Why…why is everyone staring at me?" Kingston asked concerned, wiping his mouth with the back of his fist.

With that said, Eureka cleared her throat and took the time to gather her thoughts before speaking.

"Fear, the man that helped rescue you from that British assassin…his real name is Alvin Simpson …and he's your father, baby." Eureka gave her only son the cold, hard truth.

Kingston's neck coiled and his eyelids stretched wide open. He gasped looking between his mother and the man that he was led to believe was his father. He couldn't believe what he had been told. Surely, his mother was fucking with him. He was just waiting for his father to speak up and tell him that this was all a joke. Instead, he looked down with sadness in his eyes and fidgeted with his fingers.

"Dad, is this true?" Kingston asked, scared to hear his father's response.

Clearing his throat and swallowing the lump of nervousness there, Tristan looked up at his son and nodded his response. A fresh set of tears formed in his eyes and threatened to flood his cheeks. Seeing this, Kingston knew that what his mother had said was absolutely true. It made him feel played and hurt. Shutting his eyelids for a moment, he peeled them back open and looked around disappointedly. In closing his eyes, he hoped that when he opened them that he would be inside of his bedroom and that all of this would have been a nightmare. It was unfortunate that this didn't happen and he would be forced to deal with his reality.

"But why? Why tell me this now?" Kingston asked.

"Truthfully," Eureka started, wiping her tearing eyes with her curled finger. "I was too scared of the outcome of the paternity results. Although I wanted you to have been by your father, I knew that there was a possibility that you were Fear's. It haunted me for years not knowing for sure who your biological father was. This year I finally got up the courage to get the test done so that you, me, and your father could know the truth. I'm sorry, baby. Momma is so sorry for hurting and confusing you. Please, find it in your heart to forgive me somehow, I beg of you, son." She said with her hands together pleadingly. "You're the greatest thing to have ever happen to me and to lose your love will devastate me. I am nothing without you…" She said unapologetically, eyes dripping her remorse, "Absolutely nothing."

"Is…Is all of this true?" Kingston questioned with an eyebrow raised.

"Yes, honey, everything we have told you so far is the truth. I know it's a hard pill to swallow, but I hope that you can find it in your heart to forgive us all."

"Wow," the little nigga said in astonishment, staring ahead at nothing.

In a flash, Anton chopped Eureka and Tristan at the back of her necks, putting them both out cold. Having observed his handiwork, he dragged his brother in law and his sister over to the stove where he handcuffed them to the handle of the stove. Afterwards, he stepped over them and walked over to the kitchen table where he sat down, where Kingston stared at him like he was a psycho. Anton wiped his sweaty forehead with the back of his hand and cracked an easy smile at his nephew.

"Don't worry, they'll be fine," Anton told the boy. "I just need them out for what I'm about to lay on you next." With that said, he pulled out a black Sharpie marker and drew a circle around his left peck where his beating heart was. Tossing the marker aside, he withdrew a .22 handgun from the small of his back and sat it down at the table. Leaning forward, he placed the small caliber weapon before his nephew and lay back in his chair. Afterwards, he instructed the little nigga to pick the gun up. He was hesitant at first, but he eventually picked the weapon up, looking at it and then his uncle, wondering exactly what he wanted him to do with it.

The thought popped up inside of his young mind but he tried to convince himself that that's not what his uncle had in mind.

"Uncle Ant, you want me to shoot chu?" Kingston's face balled up with confusion.

"It will all make sense in a minute."Anton assured his nephew. His shut his eyelids briefly and took a breath, preparing himself for what needed to be said. Afterwards, he peeled his eyelids open and looked his nephew in his eyes. "Your father...not Tristan...Fear. Well, he didn't just die in the fire...I left him there to die. I handcuffed him to the radiator." At that moment, Kingston's eyes lit up and his lips peeled open in surprise. The young hitta went on to tell him about the long lasting beef between him and his father. He told him how him, Eureka and Fear had met and how they had discovered that he was the one that had murdered his grandfather. Afterwards, he handed the boy the letter that Fear had given him, which revealed to him that he was the one that had knocked off his father.

Kingston looked back and forth between the letter and his uncle. His face twisted with anger and tears pooled in his eyes. The .22 was in his hand now, and he was clutching it so tight that his knuckles turned white. He suddenly shot to his feet and turned his gun sideways, pointing it at his uncle. Sitting there, staring The Grim Reaper square in his eyes, Anton didn't bat an eyelash. He'd been in the face of death more times than he cared to count. The last thing on earth he was afraid of was dying. Hell, the young nigga couldn't be in his line of work.

"I know that look in your eyes," Anton began. "It's the same one I had when I finally caught up with your father. I wanted him so badly that my dick was hard...I mean, really hard. I thought that if I took his life and avenged my old man that it would make me feel better, but unfortunately it didn't. But who knows, nephew, you may have better luck...so go ahead…give that trigger a squeeze and see if it was all worth it like I did."

Kingston stood there teary eyed huffing and puffing, finger settled on the trigger. The little nigga was trying to calm down because he was furious with anger. A million and one things raced back and forth across his young mind. He felt confusion and anger. All of this time he thought that Tristan was his father, but it turned out that the hit-man known as Fearless actually was. On top of that, this was the same bastard that his grandmother had hired to murder his grandfather for one million dollars in life insurance money. At that precise moment he couldn't help thinking that he had one big dysfunctional, psychotic family.

Still, Kingston worshipped the ground that his uncle walked on and he loved his parents beyond words. No matter how dysfunctional they were they were his family and he wouldn't trade them for the world. His immature mind couldn't even begin to fathom a life without them in it. And if there was such a life he was one hundred percent sure that he didn't want it.

Kingston shut his eyelids and tears jetted down his cheeks. Taking a deep breath, his shoulders slumped and he slowly laid his banger down on the table. When he peeled his eyelids back open, his eyes were glassy and red webbed. Using the palms of both of his hands, he ran them down his face. He licked his lips and looked his uncle in the eyes.

"I forgive you for killing my father, Uncle Anton…It hurts but I forgive you," he said, his eyes accumulating tears again. His chest jumped up and down as he breathed.

Anton was silent as he sat there, tears welling up in his eyes and then sliding down his cheeks. His nostrils flared as he breathed heavily, chest expanding and shrinking.

"I'm sorry, King. I'm very, very sorry, nephew." He spoke sorrowfully.

"I know," the boy wiped his eyes with the back of his fist and sniffled.

Anton opened his arms for a hug and said, "Come here."

Right then, Kingston took off running in his uncle's direction. He felt his strong arms wrap around him and embrace him lovingly. Face pressed against his chest, the boy sobbed and held to him tight.

"It's okay, let it alllll out…let it alllll out," Anton's hand swept up and down Kingston's back soothingly, tears dripping from his eyes.

"Uuuh," Tristan's eyelids fluttered open and he looked around. He went to rub the back of his neck where Anton had struck his pressure point and his wrist was snagged. When he looked up he saw that his wrist was shackled to the handle of the stove. Hearing sobbing, he looked to his son and his brother in law. Seeing them in the heartfelt moment brought a stinging to his pupils and he found himself getting teary eyed.

"You…you told 'em?" Hearing a feminine voice at his left, Tristan looked and found Eurcka wide awake. There were teardrops falling from her eyes as she looked on at what was going on between her brother and son.

When Anton heard his sister's emotional voice, he whipped his head around to her and found her face slicked wet. Holding her gaze, he nodded his answer to her.

"Gimmie the keys to the cuffs." Eureka told her brother. He obliged her, tossing the keys to the handcuffs. She caught the keys and hurriedly unlocked the metal bracelets that had her and her husband bound. Together, she and her significant other pulled off the handcuffs and rushed over to Anton and Kingston. They embraced in one big family group hug, crying.

Chapter Eleven

Once the jet finally landed a staircase was pushed over to the hatch. A moment later, it was opened and Raymar stepped out. He was decked out in a Grey Armani suit and black leather shoes, polished to a shine. He adjusted his tie and his cuff-links, smiling from ear to ear. He shut his eyelids and slightly tilted his head back, inhaling the air of his native land. After expelling a deep breath, he looked ahead and found two men dressed in expensive suits, ear buds in their ears, looking like a couple of secret service agents. One of them opened the back door of a stretch Mercedes Benz and stood aside, waiting for him to come down. The other kept a close watch on things, his hand near the gun holstered on his hip. Seeing that the gentlemen were waiting for him, Raymar made his way down the staircase. Having cleared the steps, he ducked off inside the back of the luxurious limousine, door shutting behind them.

Raymar rode in the backseat on the butter soft leather seats smearing caviar on Ritz crackers and indulging in the most expensive champagne that money could buy. Once he was done, two voluptuous Nigerian women that had been there all the while smoking blunts and sipping champagne started pulling off his clothing. First they unbuttoned his shirt and then they slipped off his tie. Next, came his leather shoes and slacks. The ladies kept going until the nigga was clad in his boxer briefs. Afterwards, they rolled up the patrician, sucking and fucking Raymar all of the way to his father's house.

The Mercedes pulled up to a villa that was heavily guarded. Soldiers were stationed right outside of the gates and a couple patrolled the estate holding German Shepherds on leashes, M-16 slung over their shoulders. One of the secret service agents looking dudes hopped out of the front passenger seat and opened the back door, holding it ajar for the occupant. Raymar stepped out of the car wearing red lip stick imprints on his face and neck, zipping up his slacks and buckling his belt. He looked up at his father's home as the door of the limousine was being shut behind him. Once he'd gotten his clothing adjusted, Raymar was allowed to enter the gates, escorted by one of the dudes that had picked him up when the jet had landed. The maid opened the front door of the villa and escorted him to his father's study. It was there that he found him standing at his desk and staring at a portrait. The photo inside of the frame was on him, his late wife and a young Raymar. When Nero heard his son enter his domain, he sat the portrait down on his desk top and dabbed his tearing eyes with his handkerchief. Raymar frowned when he saw his father crying. He'd never saw him shed a tear for as long as he'd been alive. Hell, he believed he wasn't capable of crying the way he carried on and shit. But it appeared to him now that things had changed, and rightfully so.

"You okay, pop?" Raymar asked concerned.

Nero, still dabbing his tearing eyes, looked up like he'd just noticed his son standing there. Quickly, he stuffed his handkerchief where he'd gotten it and limped towards Raymar as fast as he could, tears still rolling down his cheeks. He threw the arm that was holding his cane around his shoulders and broke down sobbing.

"What's…what's wrong, pop?" Raymar worried.

Nero swallowed the spit in his throat and sniffled, gathering himself before he spoke. "My…my baby boy, I thought that I'd never see you again…" he cried and kissed him on the side of the face twice, hugging him with one arm tighter. His son hugged him tighter as well, tears pooling his eyes.

"It's…it's okay, pop. I'm here now; everything is going to be alright." He rubbed his hand up and down his old man's back, as tears ran down his own cheeks.

"I know. I know, but you gotta leave again," Nero told him.

"Leave again?" Raymar's forehead wrinkled and he broke his father's embrace. "Where am I going now?"

Snikt!

Nero unsheathed his katana which doubled as his cane, eyebrows arching and crinkles forming at the beginning of his nose. He smacked his hand down on his son's shoulder and gripped it. He drew back his sword and drove it through Raymar's chest. It came out of his back and he rose to the tips of his shoes. The Brazilian fugitive's blood ran down his father's katana, over his knuckles and dripped to the floor. Nero brought his lips to his son's ear and whispered, ever so gently, "You disgraced our family's name, Raymar." He then kissed him on his lips gently. This was 'The Kiss of Death'. The Brazilian crime boss snatched his katana out of his son and he dropped down to his knees on the floor. He looked up at his father accusingly, teardrops falling from his eyes. He held his chest, slicking his hands red with his life's blood. He watched as his father flipped his katana around in his hand as he circled him, his hateful eyes glued to him. Stopping at the front of him, he took a hold of his blade with both hands and whipped it across his neck, severing his head. Raymar's head fell off to the side and landed straight up. His body slumped backwards, palms facing upwards.

Nero took a deep breath, looking down at the mess he'd created. Eyes still focused on the corpse of his son, he whipped his handkerchief out and used it to wipe off his sword. He then flipped his son's severed head upon its skull and stabbed his katana through the bottom of it. Next, he held Raymar's head up and studied his face. His pupils were rolled to their corners and his tongue was hanging out the side of his mouth.

The Brazilian crime boss, keeping his eyes on his son's severed head, reached inside of his suit and pulled out a small flip cellular. He snapped the device open with his thumb and speed dialed someone.

"Riddihma, I have a job for you to do…"

Later that night

He stood on his knees in the field before a legion of angry men, some of whom he knew as comrades and others as enemies. As it stood, all of the hostile men were his enemies now. They all held burning torches whose flames illuminated their faces. The man at their mercy didn't have to guess how this had happened because he already knew. The son of a bitch went shooting his mouth off to Nero, telling him of the rebellion that his comrades had planned. The only reason his comrades knew was because one of the soldiers had informed them that he had gotten drunk and told him about the deal he'd cut wit Nero. According to the soldier, the snitch was promised a higher position within the Brazilian crime boss's empire and fifty thousand dollars. Homeboy thought that the deal was sweet enough for him to give up his comrades, which was why he was on his knees now with his wrists bound behind his back and a potato sack over his head, shivering.

There was a disturbance in the audience as someone moved forward in it. Finally, that someone came to the forefront. It was Goldie. Gold Mouth's little brother. The young nigga looked exactly like his older sibling, only he was slender and had short dreadlocks. He had a burning torch in one hand and an AK-47 slung over his shoulder. His eyebrows were arched and he clenched his teeth, showcasing the shiny gold grill inside of his mouth. The side of his face was illuminated by the golden orange flames of the torch that he held at his shoulder. Reaching forth, he yanked off the potato sack and revealed the identity of the rat within their pack. It was Lupe. He had a gag stretched across his mouth. Carved in his forehead in bold letters was the word 'Rat.' His face was bruised black and blue, his eyelid was swollen shut and his nose was as big as a pickle. The collar of his white T-shirt was stained pink from his blood sliding down his neck and soiling it.

Staring down at his former comrade with utter disgust, Goldie watched as tears burst from his eyes and dripped down onto the dirt.

"Do you know you're one sorry ass, back stabbing, piece of stinking shit, Lupe? You gave this union your ass to kiss and now we're gonna give you ours." When Goldie finished his statement, one of the men standing with him doused Lupe with gasoline and he touched his torch to his chest, just as he went to plead for his life. He and the rest of the criminals watched in satisfaction as their former ally withered on the ground. Before they knew it the fire had burned away the gag in his mouth and the duct-tape that had his wrists bound. Once these restraints had been disintegrated, Lupe hollered out in excruciation and thrashed around on the dirt.

Keeping his eyes on a burning, thrashing Lupe, Goldie gave the order to one of his little homies to finish him off.

"Caesar, relieve him of his pain." He said with unforgiving eyes.

With the command given, a little dude about sixteen years of age stepped forth. He was in a dingy T-shirt and filthy, tattered jeans. He pulled out a Colt .45 revolver and squeezed the trigger twice. The chamber twisted and fire spat from its barrel, causing Lupe's skull to jerk with each shot that penetrated it. Caesar allowed his pistol to linger in the air as he stared at his handiwork for a moment before stashing his warm revolver into the front of his raggedy jeans.

"Change of plans, we move on Nero tonight, two days ahead of schedule." Goldie told the other criminals that had united to take a stand against the Brazilian crime boss.

At this time, the crack of dawn was upon them and the sky was a navy blue. The criminals jumped into their vehicles and drove back in the opposite direction. As they drove ahead they saw two florescent orbs moving towards them. The orbs suddenly stopped and the criminals discovered that they were headlights. They watched as the front passenger door of what appeared to be an old F-150 truck opened and a short man hopped out, ski-mask over his face to conceal his identity. An AK-47 was slung over his shoulder. He had a hefty, lumpy bag of something in one hand and a fist full of long, sharpened sticks. Frowns crossed Goldie and his comrades' faces as they observed the short man stab a total of four sticks into the ground. He then went down the row of sticks with the hefty bag, removing large oval shaped objects from out of it and pressing them down onto the sharpened sticks that he planted into the surface.

Once he had pressed the last object down on the last stick, he patted the top of it and walked away. Grabbing a hold of the passenger door, he looked up at the oncoming cars heading in his direction. He froze for a moment before hopping into the front passenger seat and slammed the door shut. He stuck his hand out of the window and patted the roof of the truck. The driver threw the F-150 into drive and pulled off.

Seeing the old heap pull off, Goldie and his men drove faster to see what was left out at the end of the field. The further they drove out the higher the sun rose into the air until the orange reddish marble was posted over the field. Goldie and his comrades' vehicles skidded to a halt before the sticks the short man had planted in the ground, causing dust to go up in the air. The doors of the respective vehicles swung open and the criminals hopped out, walking towards the sticks. Stopping where they were, they looked upon the objects that were pressed down on the ends of the sticks. They were actually the severed heads of Raphael, Gold Mouth, Keno and Raymar. The eyes of the heads were rolled to their corners and their mouths were hanging open, tongues hanging out of their mouths.

Just then, a flock of pigeons soared high above the field. The bird that stood out among the flock was white and covered in large brown spots. Its wings were expanded to its full potential as it glided across the sky, making those noises that all of the feathery creatures make. It wasn't long before it defecated, sending its pasty white shit plummeting towards the ground.

Splat!

The pigeon's shit splattered on the face of Raymar's severed head. It was followed by several more droplets of shit, which splattered on his nose and lips. The birds flew off into the distance, making their noises like only they could.

Coo! Coo! Coo! Coo!

Horror was etched on the faces of Goldie and his comrades as they exchanged glances. In that moment, they realized that Nero was the boss of all bosses of Rio and he wasn't the nigga that they wanted to fuck with. Murdering off their leaders was one thing, but to whack out his only son. Well, that was some certified gangsta shit that they didn't want any parts of.

That night

A black Ford Suburban on chrome "24 rims pulled up at a huge mansion and its driver killed its engine. The driver side door swung open and the chauffeur jumped out. After adjusting his cuff-links he made his way around to the opposite side of the SUV and opened the door. A Timberland boot stepped out into view first, and then the roach end of a blunt was dropped to the ground. The litterer's hand grasped the armrest of the door panel and he hopped out. He was a rather short fellow with a fade that swirled with waves. He had a five o'clock shadow and a muscular form that filled out a black thermal and matching Levi's that hung slightly off of his ass. He took in his surroundings as he blew smoke from his nostrils and mouth. Next, he hoisted the strap of the duffle bag over his shoulder that he'd pulled out of the transporting vehicle. The chauffeur shut the door behind his passenger and posted up holding his wrists at his waist.

"Fear!"

The fellow looked up hearing his name being called. He couldn't quite see who it was standing out on the porch of the mansion, so he held his stump above his brows. There was a nasty, ugly scar there from where he had removed it. The scar would be there forever, reminding him of the fight of his life. Peering closely, Fear finally made out the man, who was leaning his weight on a cane.

"'Sup with it, OG?" he lowered his stump and walked towards Nero.

Flashback

Fear's eyes prowled the floor of the burning mansion looking for something that he could use to remove the chain of the handcuff that bound him to the radiator. His pupils stopped when they landed on a saw. He lay on his stomach and tried reaching for it but it was out of his reach. Having realized this, he tried to pull the tool closer with his foot. He managed to lift it slightly from off of the floor by the heel of his boot, but he couldn't pull it any closer. Hearing the roaring fire and more of the ceiling crashing to the floor somewhere in the distance, he knew that he had better act fast before he found himself being burned alive.

Fear's body was warm and he was sweating profusely. Using the back of his hand, he wiped the beads of sweat that had accumulated on his forehead. Next, he untied his right boot and removed its lace. He tied the lace at the last hole of the boot and lay on his stomach, like he did when he was trying to grasp the saw with his hand. Cocking his arm back, he threw the boot forward and missed the handle of the saw by an inch; he repeatedly this act twice before taking a deep breath and trying again. Bingo! He smiled when his boot landed on the handle of the saw. At this time, his cell phone was ringing with back to back calls from Eureka, but his freedom had his undivided attention. Slowly, he pulled the saw into him and picked it up. Holding it up at his shoulder, he smiled triumphantly and kissed the rusty blade. He placed the blade to his shackle and went about the task of sawing it off, but the edges of the tool wouldn't cut through the metal. This caused his brows to furrow and his heart to drop into the pit of his stomach. The triumphant smile drained from his face and he continued to try to cut through the shackle with the saw.

"Aaaaaah!" He threw his head back and hollered aloud, veins bulging at his temples. He looked at his arm and saw that he had been burned. The fire was hastily closing him in. He scooted away as far as he could from the flames and tried cutting through the shackle again, but he still didn't have any luck. Defeated, he sat the saw down and crossed himself in the sign of the crucifix, figuring that he was about to die. Bowing his head, he began to recite a prayer that his mother had taught him when he was a little boy. Both of his parents were very religious, so he was brought up in church. Although he didn't adhere to the Christian faith, he still believed in a higher power and he hoped that whoever it was would see him fit to spare from death.

Fear peeled his eyelids open after reciting his prayer. He looked to the shackle around his wrist and saw the red lines that had formed there from him yanking on the handcuff. His yanking had left red impressions there that were the image of his shackle. He looked from the shackle to the saw, with its dull edges. A light bulb came on inside of his head and he picked the saw back up. He looked back and forth between it and his shackle. The edges of the tool weren't sharp enough to cut through metal, but it may be sharp enough to cut through flesh. His flesh! Having bit down on his boot, Fear placed the saw to his wrist and took a deep breath. His heart thudded inside of his chest as he stared at the saw pressed against his wrist. Shutting his eyelids briefly, he built up enough courage to proceed with what he had in mind.

Fear pushed the saw forward against his wrist and the meat there ripped open, blood dotting his face. Wrinkles formed on his forehead and around his nose and he bit down on his boot harder, continuing to saw off his hand. He moved the saw back and forth, dotting his face with more blood and pelting the floor with it also. He growled and his face wrinkled more, steadily sawing into the bone of his wrist. Blackish red blood seemed to flow in a stream the more he continued sawing, dotting his face with more and more blood. His eyes rolled up into the back of his head he was losing so much blood. He almost fainted from blood loss, but his determination egged him on. Before Fear knew it, his wrist came loose from his hand and he fell backwards, hollering so loud that the thing at the back of his throat vibrated.

Fear took the time to calm himself down as best as he could, closing his eyelids briefly and swallowing the spit in his throat. When he peeled his eyelids back open, he saw a black device on Anton's utility belt beeping with a red flashing light. Right then, he knew that it was an explosive attached to the belt. With no time to lose, Fear took off running towards the kitchen, running through fire and shit unscathed. He kicked the backdoor off of its hinges and it crashed to the ground, his form rolling forward on the lawn. By the time he got to his feet, the mansion was exploding and he was running towards the pool of filthy brown water. The first explosion was small but the next one sent his ass high into the air, pitching him forward. He hurled back down towards the pool, making a big ass splash upon impact of the surface of the water. The flames of the explosion rushed forward, missing him. A few moments later, Fear's broke the surface of the water, breathing hard and looking around. Wincing, he pulled himself from out of the pool and scaled the fence with his good hand. Coming around on the other side, he jumped down and ran down the alley, trickling blood along the way.

***

Boom!
Fear kicked open the double doors of the restaurant and startled the patrons. They all looked to him in shock but he

didn't give a mad ass fuck. He had to do something to stop from bleeding to death. His eyes scanned his surroundings and he spotted a bust boy coming from out of the twin doors of the kitchen. Quickly, he took off running towards the kitchen. People got the fuck out of his way, not wanting to be involved in any of the shit the killa may have going on. Bursting through the twin doors of the kitchen, Fear looked all around and saw the kitchen staff dressed in all white. The steam from the grills and dish water rose into the air. Oddly, everyone was occupied with what they were doing and weren't paying him any mind. When Fear spotted one of the chefs cooking a pot of something hot on one of the stoves, he took off in his direction. He shoved him out of the way and smacked the big ass pot from off of the stove. It felt to the ground and made a loud clasp, its contents spilling out onto the floor. The kitchen staff moved out of the way to avoid the hot soup in the pot.

Fear took three deep breaths before bringing his stump to the flames of the burner of the stove. He hollered so loud this time that he felt himself going hoarse and tears outlined his eyelashes. It hurt like a son of a bitch, but he had to do it if he wanted to stay alive. Taking his stump away from the flames, Fear turned around to the kitchen staff smiling. He took about three steps before he collapsed to the floor, fading to black.

Sometime later, Fear stirred awake inside of the hospital having had a blood transfuse Mon. It was then that he was grateful to whomever that had made sure he made it to the hospital in time.

Present

Eureka and her family believed that Fear was dead and he decided to leave it that way. He thought it was in his best interest that they believed that he was deceased. This was because he knew what kind of life he led and he didn't have any plans of leaving it any time soon. He knew in his heart that he was doing the right thing. You couldn't tell him that he wasn't. There wasn't any doubt in his mind that Tristan would make the perfect father figure for his son. The Dominican man was all about family and he loved Eureka and Kingston unconditionally. With him out of the picture, he was sure that they could lead a life of happiness. He could sleep better at night knowing this.

"Business as usual, glad you could make it." Nero shook the killa's hand.

"Shiiit, as much money as you're breaking me off, I'd be a fool not to show up. You feel me?" he cracked a smile as he shook his hand, "Where's my men?"

"They're in the back." He threw his head towards the mansion, referring to the backyard, "One hundred men in total."

"Alright. You lead the way," Fear adjusted the strap of the duffle bag on his shoulder and followed the Brazilian crime boss inside of his home.

Nero led Fear through the kitchen to the back door, which he opened and stepped aside. The killa stepped through the door where he found the one hundred men that he was paid the sum of $200,000 dollars to train. These men were a third of Nero's army and they were all criminals. After he was done with giving them the knowledge that he obtained through his sensei's teachings, he'd go on to teach the next batch of men and so on and so forth. He was paid to teach these men any and everything that he knew about the art of murder, just like he had taught Eureka and Anton. This was by far the largest group of people that he had ever had to teach, but he was sure that he was up for the task. Nero had pulled Fear off of the streets because of his handicap, and he figured that this was an acceptable way for him to earn a living.

Fear took in all of the faces of the men he was given to train; all of them had hard faces. They were also all dressed in T-shirts and cargo pants. The killa nodded in approval of the men standing before him. Seeing that he had all of their attention, he introduced himself and told them that he would be training them for a month, and that it would indeed be the most vigorous exercises that they have ever participated in. Afterwards, he called for a chair and Nero's butler brought him out one. He unzipped his duffle bag and pulled out rope, which he made into a noose. He then sat the chair underneath the shade of a tree. Having tossed the duffle bag aside, Fear threw the noose over the tree's branch and tied the other end around a nearby tree. He stood upon the chair and pulled the noose down, tugging on it. Once he was sure that it was secure, he hopped off of the chair. He stepped before his men rubbing his hands together, noticing that they all were looking at him and the noose strangely.

"Alright, who's going first?" Fear looked around at all of the men.

The men exchanged whispers and glances.

"Wait a minute. You expect us to let chu hang us from a fuckin' tree?" a young man with a caramel complexion inquired. He was slender with bleached blonde hair that had been pushed up by his black roots. "You must be out cho goddamn mind." He scowled and folded his arms across his chest.

The men talked in hushed tones among themselves and agreed with homie with the bleached blonde hair.

"I feel you, youngin', it sounds stupid," Fear told him, rolling up the sleeve of his thermal and revealing more of his stump. "But if you gone be in the murder game then you can't be afraid to die. Nah, you see, you gotta be able to look death in its eyes and laugh at it; tell that cock sucker to suck your dick, you feel me?"

Flashback

Fear threw the noose over the tree's branch and tied the other end around a nearby tree. He stood upon the chair and pulled the noose down, tugging on it. Once he was sure that it was secure, he hopped off of the chair. He stepped before Eureka and Anton rubbing his hands together.

"Alright, whose going first?" his eyes shifted from Eureka to Anton.

Anton raised an eyebrow as he looked from the idling noose to Fear. He gave him the side eye and twisted his lips.

"My dude, I know you don't think I'ma 'bout to hang myself from no mothafucking tree?" Anton folded his arms across his chest, looking at Fear like 'Nigga, you can't be serious.' "No way no how, that ain't happening."

"If you're gonna be in this game then you can't be afraid to die." Fear told them. "You gotta be able to look death in its eyes and laugh at it; tell that cock sucker to suck your dick, you feel me?"

"This ain't the 1920s and I ain't looking to be lynched."

Fear took a deep breath and exhaled. Hands to together, he stepped before Anton.

"Baby boy, this is the first step in your training, if you can't do this then step off." Fear pointed a crooked finger beyond him. "You try your luck out there with the boy Malvo and see how you come out."

"Fuck it. That's what it is then." Anton shrugged and was about to walk off until Eureka stepped in his path, outstretching an arm across his chest.

"We'll do it and I got first." Eureka told Fear.

"Reka," Anton frowned.

She whipped around, eyebrows arched.

"Don't Reka me, you wanted in this life. Well, here it is." She told him. "I'm not going back to the streets, baby boy. There ain't nothing there for you or me. You with me?" she held out her hand.

He looked down at her hand thinking for a moment and then he responded, "Yeah."

They gave one another a complex handshake and she stepped over to Fear. He directed her toward the chair and she stepped upon it, both feet planted firmly on the seat. Grabbing the chair about the back, he stepped upon it and brought the noose down, looping it around her neck. He then jumped down. He and Anton looked up at her as if she was on the Empire State building. Eureka stared straight ahead, taking deep breaths to prepare her for what she'd gotten into. Using his red bandana, Fear tied her hands behind her back and stood off to the side of her.

"You sure you wanna go through with this?" Anton questioned, he got a bad feeling about her being hung up like that from a tree. The whole idea was stupid to him but he loved her without a fault. She was his sister and his best friend and he'd follow her to the end of earth.

Eureka continued to stare straight ahead as she nodded. She listened to Fear as he talked, his voice coming from the left of her.

"Alright, on the count of three I'm going to kick this chair from under you, okay?" he asked. She nodded and took two deep breaths, blinking her eyes. "Okay. One...Two..." he kicked the chair from underneath her feet before the count of three, taking her and Anton completely off guard. Her body hurled toward the ground but the rope yoked that mothafucka right back up. She dangled from side to side, eyes growing moist and legs thrashing the air wildly. Her face quickly reddened and veins formed on her temples.

"What the fuck, man? You said three." Anton barked on Fear, ready to whip his ass. "That was unexpected."

"Death is unexpected." Fear looked up at Eureka, struggling upon the rope. He stayed focused on her as he talked to Anton. "You wanna be a killa then you need to accept the fact that death will come for you any day. You don't get to make an appointment; that bastard just shows up and it's time for you to go."

Present

"Alright, who wants to be the first to volunteer?"Fear looked around at all of the faces of the men in the audience, holding the rope in his hand. He was about to randomly pick someone when a stocky man with a shaved head and receding hairline stuck his hand up in the air. This made Fear crack a one sided grin. He pointed to the man and said, "Ah, there we go, brave soul, come on up here, family." He motioned the man forth. Once he finally got a good look at him, he had one milky white eye and a nasty scar that traveled over his eye and extended the full length of his cheek. Fear shook homeboy's hand and stepped upon the chair, motioning for the man to step upon the chair beside him. One the man got upon the chair; Fear looped the noose around his neck and jumped down to the surface.

Shaved head stared straight ahead, taking deep breaths to prepare him for what he'd signed up for. Fear pulled a red bandana from his right back pocket and used it to tie his volunteer's hands behind his back. He then stood off to the side of him.

"You sure you're up for this?" Fear asked, staring up at him.

Shaved head continued to stare straight ahead as he nodded. He spread his legs apart and twitched his toes, making sure he was well balanced upon the seat of the chair. Afterwards, he shut his eyelids briefly and swallowed the lump of nervousness in his throat, Adams apple moving up and down his neck.

"Alright, on the count of three, I'm going to kick this chair from under you, okay?" he asked. Shaved head nodded and took a deep breath, blinking his eyelids. "Okay. One…Two…" he kicked the chair from underneath his feet before the count of three, taking him off guard.

Class is in session.

The Devil Wears Timbs V

EPILOGUE

Tristan paced back and forth outside of the bathroom door, massaging his chin. Occasionally, he'd glance at his watch but he never broke his stride. At the moment, he was on edge and anxious, waiting for Eureka to come out of the bathroom, hopefully with some good news. You see, Eureka and Tristan had been trying for a child of their own for a few months now. Although the strip club bouncer loved young Kingston with all that he was, he still wanted a child that shared his bloodline.

Stopping his pacing, Tristan reached inside of his back pocket and pulled out his wallet. Cracking it open, he pulled out a folded slip of paper. On this paper was who Eureka chose to be with out of him and Fear. He hadn't read it in eleven months because he was afraid of his wife's decision. Having finally gathered up the courage, he decided to go ahead and see who his love had chosen. Holding the paper in his hands, he took a deep breath and unfolded the paper. His hands slightly trembled as he held the paper pinched between his fingers, like it was that small piece of paper from a fortune cookie.

I love you and I choose you, Tristan Toretto.

And I'd choose you; in a hundred lifetimes, in a hundred worlds, in any version of reality, I'd find you and I'd choose you.

— Kiersten White, The Chaos of Stars

Reading these word instantly made Tristan tear up. He sniffled and licked his lips. Before he knew it, water spilled over the rims of his eyes and teardrops fell, splattering against the paper. He felt his heart swell with pride, joy, affection and love. Afterwards, he wiped his eyes with the back of his hand and took another deep breath, looking down at the words scrolled across the paper again. More tears came to his eyes and fell in droplets, pelting the paper. Finally, he folded the paper up, kissed it and stashed it into his shirt's pocket.

Hearing the bathroom door click with a twist of the doorknob, Tristan stopped dead in his tracks and turned around. He found himself face to face with a smiling Eureka; she leaped into his arms and kissed him all over his face. He smiled and dimpled his cheeks. She held up the pregnancy test and he took it. There was a blue cross in the square. She was pregnant.

"You're pregnant! Oh my God, baby," An excited Tristan kissed Eureka and spun her around and around, watching her smiling face. They fell over on the bed with her landing on top of him. They lay their staring into one another's eyes for a time, falling in love all over again. The lovers kissed romantically and then she laid her head against his chest, feeling his embrace. She shut her eyelids for a time, still wearing that beautiful smile of hers on her lips. Tristan had shut his eyelids and smiled too, rubbing his hand up and down her back.

Love is the most incredible thing in the world.

To Be Concluded in...

The Devil Wears Timbs 6

Just Like Daddy

AVAILABLE NOW BY TRANAY ADAMS

The Devil Wears Timbs 1-7

Bury Me A G 1-5

These Scandalous Streets 1-3

A South Central Love Affair

Me And My Hittas 1-6

The Last Real Nigga Alive 1-3

God Bless the Trappers 1-3

A Gangsta's Empire 1-4

Fangeance

Fear My Gangsta 1-5

A Hood Nigga's Blues

The Realest Killaz 1-3

The Last of the OGs 1-3

The Streets Don't Love Nobody 1-2

The Dopeman's Bodyguard 1-2

King of the Trenches